STOP THE WEDDING!

a romantic comedy

by STEPHANIE BOND

If anyone objects to this marriage,

let them speak now...

ISBN: 0989042901
ISBN 13: 9780989042901

Front cover by Andrew Brown at clicktwicedesign.com

CHAPTER ONE

ANNABELLE COAKLEY picked up her half-eaten sandwich to make room for a pile of folders her assistant Michaela held, then juggled the phone to her opposite ear. "Mom, I'd love to chat, but right now I'm really covered up." Mike pointed to her watch and mouthed that Annabelle was due in court in twenty minutes. Annabelle held up one finger. "Can I call you back tonight?"

A clucking sound came over the phone. "Tonight is my dance class, dear. I won't keep you, I just called to tell you I'm getting married."

Annabelle stopped mid-nod to her assistant and jammed the receiver closer to her ear. "You're what?"

"I'm getting married."

Her head felt as if it might implode. "Hold on, Mom." Annabelle covered the mouthpiece and told Mike which files she needed for court, then waved her from the cramped office. As soon as the door closed, she uncovered the phone and laughed. "With all the confusion here, I must have misunderstood. I thought you said—" she laughed again, harder, "—that you were getting *married*." She shook her head at the sheer absurdity that her sweet widowed mother would consider something so reckless.

"That's right, dear. I'm getting married."

Annabelle sobered and curled her fingers around a dagger-shaped letter opener on her desk. "To Melvin?"

"His name is Martin, dear. Martin Castleberry."

"The washed up movie star?"

Her mother sighed, making Annabelle wish she had inherited her patience. "To my generation, he's a legend."

She stabbed the letter opener into the corkboard pad on her desk calendar. "But you've only known him for what, three weeks?"

"Eight."

"Which is roughly equal to the number of times he's been married."

Another sigh. "This will be Martin's sixth marriage."

"Six, eight—after a while, why bother counting?"

"Be nice, dear."

She wanted to scream in frustration. "Mother, how could you *marry* a man you've only known for two months?"

"Martin and I knew we were meant for each other after two *hours*, dear."

"But… but—" She cast around for convincing words, then blurted the concern that lay closest to her heart. "But Dad's only been gone for a little while."

The words hung in the ensuing silence, and although Annabelle regretted the timing, she didn't regret her honesty. Finally, Belle cleared her throat delicately. "Your father has been gone for over two years, Annabelle, and I'm lonely."

Her heart wrenched and guilt settled around her shoulders like an itchy wool cape. "So come to Detroit for a little vacation."

Her mother made a dissenting noise. "The last time I visited I felt as if I were imposing. You have so many responsibilities."

Indeed, Annabelle recalled a day they'd spent shopping and her phone had rung at least two dozen times. She closed her eyes amidst surging regret. "Then I'll come to Atlanta more often."

"You know I'd love to see you any time. And I was hoping you'd be able to make it down for the ceremony."

Annabelle's heart began to pound. "You've already set a date?"

"Next Saturday," her mother sang.

"A week from tomorrow?" She struggled to keep the panic out of her voice. Martin Castleberry was at least seventy-five—a good twenty years older than her mother—and his romantic escapades were more legendary than her mother believed his movie career to be. She hadn't met the man, but she remembered how he'd dominated the tabloid headlines only a few years ago when he'd married a TV starlet forty years his junior. The May-December match-up had been

fodder to the late night comedians for a full three months—the duration of the ill-fated marriage.

The man was a laughingstock, and Annabelle had nearly fainted when her mother first revealed she was actually dating him. She had placated herself with the thought that while her mother was a beautiful woman, Castleberry would soon be distracted by even younger fare. Now she could kick herself for not nipping the flowering flirtation in the bud. She wet her lips. "Mom, let's talk about this tonight, shall we?"

"So will you be able to make it down for the ceremony?"

The thought of watching her good-hearted, naive, lonely mother vow to love, honor, and cherish a playboy like Martin Castleberry made her skin crawl—Belle's sweet loyal heart would be trampled when he moved on to another dalliance, and she'd experienced enough heartache the last two years. Loath to pile on more at the moment, Annabelle forced cheer into her voice. "I wouldn't miss it."

"And will you be my maid of honor?"

Annabelle flinched. "Of course."

"Oh, thank you, dear! The ceremony will be a small affair, just a few friends. Martin suggested that we say our vows by candlelight."

She rolled her eyes. "How...romantic."

"I know how busy you are, so I assume you'll fly in the day of the ceremony?"

Her teeming court docket flashed through her mind. "I'll have to check my calendar and get back to you, Mom." A glance at her watch brought her to her feet. "Speaking of which, I need to run. I'll call you later, okay? I love you."

Annabelle returned the handset and jogged across the room, her mind spinning. June might be a popular month for weddings, but no one knew better than she that it was also a popular month for divorces. Maybe the uncommonly warm weather they were experiencing inflamed domestic tempers, but it seemed that every disadvantaged woman in Detroit wanted a divorce and needed the assistance of her office. With the caseload she carried, she would be hard-pressed to spare a weekend for *paradise*, much less to witness the union of Belle Coakley and Martin Castleberry.

She shook her head and expelled a long breath. In this day and age of disposable relationships, why on earth would anyone *want* to be married?

Annabelle yanked the strap of her brimming briefcase over her shoulder, then her gaze settled upon a picture of her parents on the top of a bookshelf. With her throat tight, she lifted the silver frame and ran a finger over their smiling faces. When she'd taken the photo, who could have predicted it would be the last time they would all be together?

Her parents had built a steadfast marriage on old-fashioned values and traditional roles—relics of today's society. Belle had stayed home, cooking and cleaning and gardening and mothering Annabelle. Her father had worked long hours at a small law firm on the outskirts of Atlanta, providing a middle-class living while managing to attend most of her weekend swim meets in high school. After Annabelle graduated college, her father had been looking forward to retirement, but a heart attack had claimed him weeks shy of his goal. Later, Annabelle had wondered if he'd suspected his health was failing, because of a peculiar request he'd made of her on one of their last outings.

Anna, promise me you'll look after your mother if something happens to me. She's so vulnerable.

Of course, Dad. You know you don't even have to ask.

Losing her beloved father at twenty-six had given her insight into a house having its foundation ripped out from under its joists. Mindful of her promise to her father, she'd foregone a term of law school at the University of Michigan to help tie up the loose ends of his estate. She remembered thinking how fortunate that her parents' property had appreciated so much in value—developers were building posh neighborhoods all around their house, which had once been considered rural.

Little did she realize the imposing structure built directly behind her mother's home housed the lecherous Martin Castleberry.

Annabelle swallowed past the lump in her throat. How miserably she'd honored her father's request. Her stingy visits and phone calls had driven her mother into the arms of a notorious playboy. Her eyes narrowed as she imagined the silver-haired, perpetually tanned Castleberry with his arm looped around the shoulder of a buxom pinup. The man wasn't good enough to stand in her mother's shadow. Her blood pressure ballooned.

A perfunctory knock on her door preceded Michaela opening the door. "Annabelle, your cab is waiting, and your real estate agent is on the phone. Are you okay?"

She drew in a long, deep breath and the detached underwire in her bra gouged her rib. What did the fact that she didn't have time to buy new underwear say about her life? "I'm fine," she said, her voice surprisingly strong as she replaced the picture frame. "Do me a favor, Mike?"

"Sure."

"Clear my calendar for next week."

The woman's eyebrows climbed. "A whole week? Family emergency?"

No way was Martin Castleberry going to drag her mother's—and her own—name through the mud. She'd simply fly to Atlanta and expose him for the promiscuous thrill-seeker he was, then whisk her mother back to Detroit to live with her. Annabelle lifted her chin. "Yes. I have to stop a wedding."

Clay Castleberry used a laser pointer to indicate the last and most impressive spike on the chart. "As you can see, over the last eight years, the Munich-Tyre Venture Fund has outperformed the Dow Jones Industrial Average by six to nine percent." He paused to allow the French interpreter to translate, double-checking every intonation for the appropriate emphasis. "My partners and I predict—" At the sound of a timid knock on the door, he turned and bit back a reprimand as the receptionist stuck her head inside the dimly lit meeting room.

"Mr. Castleberry, there is a Mr. Jacobson on the telephone for you."

"Tell him I'm in a meeting, and please take a message."

"I did, sir, but he said it is urgent."

Alarm seeped into his chest as his mind jumped from one tragic reason to another why his father's friend would be placing an urgent phone call to him in Paris. He murmured, "Excuse me," then strode from the room, blinking to adjust to the bright light of the reception area. His heart thudded in his ears as he grabbed the phone on the desk and pushed the flashing button. "Jake, what's up?"

"Sorry to bother you, Clay, but I'm about to board a plane for New Zealand. I'll be out of touch for a while and I wanted to talk to you before I left."

"So Dad's all right?"

"What? Oh, yeah, Martin's going to outlive us all, the rogue."

Clay's shoulders eased with relief, but tensed again when Jacobson emitted the long whistling sound that Clay had come to recognize as a prelude to breaking the news of one of his father's shenanigans. He glanced back toward the room full of wealthy international investors he'd left hanging, and massaged the bridge of his nose. "What did he do this time?"

"He's getting married."

Clay cursed. "Not *again.*"

"Afraid so. Your father does seem to possess an odd affinity for matrimony."

Like father, nothing at all like son. "Who the devil is it this time, and please tell me she's of legal age."

"Her name is Belle Coakley. He told me she's a neighbor of his, but he clammed up when I asked her age. I thought maybe you'd met her."

Clay's mouth tightened. "No, Dad hasn't mentioned her, and I haven't been to his place in a while." They scarcely got along over the phone, much less in person. The twenty miles between their houses in Atlanta might as well be twenty thousand. "I'm sure this Coakley woman is some little starry-eyed wannabe who's caught wind of the settlement check for back royalties on *Streetwise.*"

Jake made a sympathetic sound. "Martin was robbed on that film. After all your hard work to get the money he deserved, Clay, I'd hate to see it go down the drain. Which is why I'm going back on my word, because he specifically asked me not to tell you about the wedding."

"Did he think I wouldn't find out?"

"He plans to have the ceremony before you return to Atlanta. A week from tomorrow."

Clay's head fell forward and he groaned. "Do you think he's going senile, Jake?"

"Unfortunately, no, I think he's in complete control of his faculties."

A sad statement, Clay acknowledged wryly.

A muffled voice sounded in the background. "That's my boarding call. I hate to break bad news and run, but—"

"Go, Jake, have a good time. And thanks for letting me know."

"Do you have a plan?"

Clay's mind skimmed over the business he'd probably lose by returning to the States to deal with his father's latest fiasco, and his blood boiled. "Sure. I'll simply expose this Coakley co-ed for the gold-digger she is. And—" He banged the top of the desk with his palm. "I'll do whatever it takes to stop the wedding."

CHAPTER TWO

"I LANDED, BUT MY LUGGAGE DIDN'T," Annabelle muttered into her cell phone. One thing was certain—she could no longer postpone that shopping trip for new underwear.

Michaela offered a sympathetic groan. "Did you pack a change of clothes in your carry-on?"

"There wasn't much extra room in my computer bag."

"You took your laptop?" Her friend hummed in disapproval. "I thought this was supposed to be a mother-daughter bonding visit."

"I brought some briefs with me to read, and I told my real estate agent I'd be checking e-mail—we still have to set a date for closing on my house."

"By the way, she sent a picture and a plot survey to the office. I'm consumed with jealousy—how can you afford such a great place?"

Despite their solid friendship, Annabelle was unwilling to divulge certain aspects of her personal life. "Let's just say I choose my friends and my investments wisely."

"I'm flattered. Have you called your mother?"

"No."

Her friend laughed. "You're simply going to show up on the doorstep?"

"Just think of how happy she'll be to see me."

"You're afraid they'll elope if your mother knows you're coming?"

"Okay, I'm busted. But if things go well, I'll be back in a few days, hopefully with my mother in tow. I think she just needs a change of scenery for a while. On the phone last night she told me she *loved* the guy. Ha! Can you imagine?" In the stretch of silence, she detected a lecture in the making and braced herself.

"Annabelle, are you sure you know what you're doing?"

She exhaled. "I'm sure my mother is vulnerable and on the verge of making a huge mistake."

Michaela cleared her throat. "I don't suppose this would be a good time to point out that Mrs. Coakley might not consider her daughter, a twenty-eight-year-old unmarried *divorce attorney*, to be an authority on romantic relationships."

"Mike, I have more dating experience than my mother."

"If you say so," Mike said, her voice doubtful. "But how many proposals have you collected?"

Annabelle frowned. "You know what I think about marriage."

"My point exactly. Which is why I'm saying that if you're not careful with your cynicism, you might come across as patronizing."

"I have to hang up now."

"Okay, I can take a hint. From now on I'll keep my opinions to myself."

Annabelle laughed. "No you won't."

"You're right. But good luck, and check in occasionally."

Returning the receiver, Annabelle heaved a sigh, then scanned the parade of overhead signs. With its many concourses and constant intercom pages in all languages, the Atlanta Hartsfield-Jackson International Airport could be overwhelming to visitors, but the hustle and bustle sent a warm surge of familiarity to her chest. Despite the task ahead of her, she had a sentimental spot for Atlanta. In fact, she'd always imagined she'd find her way back after law school, but the job opportunity in Detroit family services had spoken to her—especially the part about the state repaying her school loans in return for a two-year stint. One year down, and one to go.

At first she'd been appalled at her exposure to the underbelly of family disputes, but the occasional moral victories had made the struggle worthwhile. And in the process of dealing with other people's problems, she had gained enormous internal strength. She rejected Michaela's assertion that she'd grown cynical where relationships were concerned—she was simply realistic. Statistics didn't lie. Thankfully, she had stumbled upon a simple solution to her dating dilemma: She didn't. And she was suspicious of those who did.

As for her mother, well...Belle was obviously suffering a lost-partner empty-nest mid-life crisis.

Annabelle turned in the direction of ground transportation, then swung her computer bag to her shoulder and started walking. To save money, she could ride the Marta train as far north as the rail had progressed since she'd last visited, then take a cab to her childhood home. She was saving the recent windfall she'd received to split between a down payment on a house and a decent used car for her mother. Otherwise, her budget remained fairly tight, and the last-minute ticket had set her back a few paces. She hoped the airline found her luggage soon, because she couldn't afford new clothes, and she couldn't spend the next two weeks in her travel garb of roomy denim overalls, pink T-shirt, and thick-soled sandals.

The first blast of early summer heat hit her as she climbed out of the stairwell up to the train platform. A few strands of her dark hair had escaped the haphazard clip she preferred on non-work days, and her split ends tickled her nose. She fingered the hair behind her ears, then donned her yellow-lensed sunglasses against the intense glare bouncing off the concrete. Sunny and H-O-T.

Annabelle smiled—welcome to Atlanta.

When the train ground to a halt at the station, she joined the crowd pressing forward, then dropped into a hard seat facing backward. People spread out to maintain their personal distance, the doors slid closed, and the train shimmied forward. The cross section of passengers ran the gamut, from tattooed college kids to wide-eyed tourists to stoic professionals. Annabelle loved to people-watch and weave a story about the characters based on their body language.

The petite brunette ignoring her rowdy kids was wondering what had happened to her marriage. The elderly couple sitting close had arrived for a visit with their grandchildren. And the stone-faced businessman drumming his fingers on his expensive watch wanted to be somewhere else—with his lover?

She squinted. No, his dark features were too hard-edged for him to be thinking about anything remotely romantic. His olive-colored suit and white shirt were duly crisp, but the knot of his tie sagged and his black eyes and jaw were shadowed with jet-lag. He stared slightly to his left, out the plexi-glass window, but she suspected he saw none of the blurred scenery. The unshaven man wasn't on his way to a meeting—maybe a funeral? Her imagination took root and flowered. Yes, he'd come home to attend a funeral. A funeral for someone he wasn't close to, but should have been.

He glanced her way and caught her staring. The intensity of his expression sent a tickle of feminine awareness up the back of her neck. Annabelle swallowed, but couldn't bring herself to look away. Satan himself couldn't have been more compelling. His large nose, strong jaw and heavy brows were assembled in a way that would make a photographer keep walking, but cause an artist to pause. He sat a head taller than most men, and his wide shoulders spilled his frame into the empty connected seat. He looked vaguely familiar, although she was sure they'd never met. She might have asked, but the man wore his dark features like a caution sign: Approach at Your Own Risk.

He flicked his gaze over her, giving no more deliberation to her face than to her clothing, but stopping when he reached her feet. With much effort, she resisted curling under her toes to hide them. Two days ago, in an effort to connect with a fourteen-year-old witness who'd locked herself into a bathroom stall, Annabelle had suggested an impromptu dual pedicure with blue nail polish that rolled out of the girl's backpack. The strategy had worked, and since her conservative pumps had concealed the deed, Annabelle hadn't yet bothered to remove the stuff.

The man's mouth twitched down at the corners before he looked back to the window, once again preoccupied. Embarrassment bolted through her. She'd been stared down by some of the most intimidating judges and attorneys in Detroit, but she'd never felt more completely dismissed in a seconds-long look. Whatever the man did for a living, he was either a miserable failure or a phenomenal success.

Or more likely, a miserable success.

She forced her attention elsewhere through the next few stops, but she was mindful of his presence a mere six feet away, through both her peripheral vision and something that could best be described as colliding energy fields. The man's aura clobbered everything in its path, commanding regard even when his focus was elsewhere. Unnerved and flushed, she kept her gaze glued on a movie poster scribbled with graffiti.

The man rose as the train slowed at the financial district station, then picked up a black leather duffel bag in one hand, an extra-deep briefcase in the other. From the corner of her eye, she noted that he allowed everyone else to disembark before he stepped out. But she recognized his cool politeness as a power ploy. She had studied people's actions enough to know that the most influential, the most commanding figures always exited rooms and elevators last—a symbolic attempt to maintain their power by protecting their back, in her opinion. He strode away, head high, feet knowing, and took the first few steps two at a time, disappearing up into the stairwell.

After the doors slid closed, the air inside the train seemed to collapse in the man's absence, but Annabelle released a sigh of relief. She'd hate to tangle with the likes of him in a courtroom. *Or in a bedroom*, her infuriatingly hyperactive mind whispered.

When the swaying ride north resumed, she pushed the image of the unsettling stranger from her mind, noting subtle and drastic changes to the landscape. Identifying progressive areas of the city was as simple as looking for mounds of orangey-red clay where the earth had been turned in preparation for homes and roads and malls. Downtown Atlanta and the metro area were an economically prosperous mix of gray and green, concrete and trees.

Remembering the man's fleeting appraisal, Annabelle repaired her scant makeup and random hairstyle as much as possible with a mirror the size of a matchbook, and pondered how to best approach the situation ahead. Blame lay heavy on her heart for Belle's impromptu decision to marry. If she'd spent more time with her mother after her father's death, if she'd visited more often, if she'd encouraged her to sell their old high-maintenance house, Belle wouldn't have met and been taken in by Martin Castleberry. And since her neglect had contributed to the situation, it was up to her to help her mother see she was on the road to certain ruin.

So should she simply sit Belle down and be brutally honest about the lunacy of marrying Martin Castleberry, or would her opposition strengthen her mother's resolve? On the other hand, if Belle's infatuation was simply a result of loneliness—as Annabelle suspected—perhaps she should use reverse psychology and feign exuberance to make her mother take a step back and analyze the situation more clearly...although doing so might stretch the limits of her own acting ability, not to mention her sanity.

By the time the train reached the end of the northern line, Annabelle had settled upon a strategy of reserved enthusiasm until she could better feel out her mother's state of mind. She left the train, exited the station and flagged down a taxi at the curb. In the few seconds it took for the car to pull to a stop, she could almost feel the freckles popping out on her nose. Hundreds of lemons in college had lessened the effects of outdoor swim meets and practices, but her skin remained susceptible. Annabelle scrubbed a knuckle over her nose and sighed. Freckles did not lend themselves to the authoritative look she needed on the job. Or to feel grown up, which always seemed harder around her mother.

During the cab ride, she practiced a hi-Mom-I-was-just-in-the-neighborhood greeting, but was admittedly a bit nervous by the time the cab pulled up to the familiar white house with red shutters. Her heart pounded as she tipped the driver, then she climbed out and allowed the memories to roll over her. Voices and smells and images from the past rose up to comfort her...she was home.

The driveway sat empty, but her mother had told her she'd cleaned out the garage and started parking inside. On the way up the sidewalk, Annabelle pivoted and nodded in appreciation at the magazine-worthy curb appeal of the sprawling ranch-style home. The mulch beds on either side of the stoop featured the biggest and brightest of the perennials Belle had accumulated over the years. A gray birdbath with a fairy on the pedestal sat off to the right, providing nourishment to a gaggle of butterflies. The yard was immaculate, save for a single wad of crabgrass. Annabelle stooped to uproot the offending weed, an act that had her father smiling down in approval, she was certain.

I'll take care of her, Daddy, just as I promised.

When she straightened, she caught sight of a three-story coral-colored stucco home through the trees and frowned. Martin Castleberry's house, she presumed, from her mother's description. The man probably watched her mother with a pair of binoculars before he asked her out.

Annabelle climbed the stacked-stone steps of the house she'd grown up in, noticing the same rock on the same corner of the same step was loose—just loose enough to remove and put a note behind it for her friend Lisa who'd lived in the house closest to theirs at the time. But Lisa and her family had moved to Illinois when the girls were eight years old, and Annabelle had lost count of how many times their house had changed owners, as had most of the homes in their isolated neighborhood as the developers crept closer and closer. The juxtaposition of the neighborhoods today could best be described as *Southern Living* meets *Metropolitan Home.*

She rang the doorbell and smiled wide, ready to throw open her arms and embrace her mother. A minute later she stopped smiling and rang the bell again. Where would her mother be at two o'clock in the afternoon? A heartbeat later, she bit down on her tongue in realization. Probably at her boyfriend's. Correction—her *fiancé's.* Annabelle grimaced. She had never liked that uppity complicated word. *Fiancé.* Americans had simply adopted a pronunciation from the French to sugarcoat the sticky implication of the word: Constrained. Bound. Trapped.

She lifted the shiny brass knocker and rapped it loudly. Finally she retrieved a ring of keys from her purse and unlocked the door. Thinking her mother might be in the back yard, Annabelle walked through the living room toward the kitchen. Along the way, she scrutinized the newly painted walls with a critical eye—where were all the pictures of her father? In the kitchen, she stopped and stared at the counter.

Was that a *dirty* glass? And—she rubbed her eyes—a saucer with *crumbs* on it?

Well, there was her answer—some messy person had obviously kidnapped her mother and was occupying her home.

She crossed to the sliding glass door, opened it, and stepped onto the deck her father had added a few years ago. "Mom?" The back yard was vacant, but she paused to admire the two rose arbors Belle had added since her last visit, purple Damask and Americana Red, assuming her mother's tutoring had sunk in. Her mother possessed a green thumb and the picturesque back yard reflected her considerable talent, from clusters of rare perennials to common black-eyed Susans. Annabelle scanned the staggered perimeter of waist-high shrubs that faded into a wooded area and frowned at a worn spot leading out of the lawn in the direction of the coral-colored house.

Good grief, they'd literally beaten a path to each other.

The back of the towering structure was more visible from this vantage point, as well as the tall privacy fence around what she assumed was the home's back yard. In addition to sheer size, vast Palladian windows and copper roof accents set the house apart from those on her mother's street.

"Mom? It's me," she called tentatively, but was almost relieved when she heard no answer—she preferred talking to her mother alone before meeting the infamous Mr. Castleberry.

Knowing her mother would probably return soon, she retraced her steps and turned on the shower in the bath closest to her old room. While the water warmed, she walked into her mother's bathroom in search of a robe, but instead of Belle's usual cotton shifts and quilted housecoats, she could find only silky kimono-style robes. Short ones. Glaring at the rainbow collection, she chose the most modest garment in the group, a mid-thigh turquoise wrap-around number, and padded back to the shower.

When the thought crossed her mind that her mother's lingerie selection was more extensive than her own, Annabelle squeezed her eyes shut and scrubbed her scalp harder.

Clay unlocked the door to his loft condo and keyed in the password to the security alarm. The odors of fresh paint assailed him and he groaned—he'd forgotten he'd contracted to have his condo painted while he was in Paris. Two stepladders, several five-gallon drums of paint, and miles of drop cloths littered the hallway.

His lower back ached from the prolonged plane ride, and his eyes felt gritty. He set his gym bag and briefcase on the floor, then stretched and yawned. The thought of catching a few winks in his own bed sounded wonderful, but he resisted the temptation, stripping his suit on the way to the shower. Unpleasant business was best taken care of quickly, he could sleep later. For an extra jolt of alertness, he stepped inside the glass and chrome stall while the water still ran cold.

He grunted at the almost painful rush, then lathered his jaw and shaved. His father had made a living on the image of a rebel with a perpetual two-day-old stubble, and with too many of his father's features for his own comfort, he wasn't about to give anyone added cause to compare the two of them. Damn his father—why couldn't the man be like normal seventy-five-year-olds: puttering around a garden, begging for grandchildren, walking in the shopping mall every morning before it opened to the public.

He smiled wryly as he soaped his chest. His father would definitely die kicking. Clay only hoped the circumstances wouldn't be scandalous enough for the press to serve up with a juicy headline.

Refreshed, he dressed in country club casual clothes. Jeans would have been a welcome change after days of suits, but he knew his performance would be more effective in nicer clothing. While shining his shoes, he phoned directory assistance and gave the name 'Belle Coakley.' After a mechanical pause, he was rewarded with the woman's street address and phone number. Clay then called his bank and arranged to withdraw twenty thousand dollars. He'd never had to pay more than ten thousand for one of his father's lovers to take a hike, but since the proposed bride was a neighbor, he might have to foot the bill for a summer vacation far from Atlanta.

Clay unearthed his car key and exited by the door to the parking garage. He hadn't moved the Mercedes in over a month. In fact, except for infrequent treks to his father's house and occasional dinner dates, he walked everywhere, or drove his black quad-cab pickup. A shame, he decided as he unlocked the door to the silver sedan, since it was 'such a nice ride'—as his last dinner date had declared at least five times before they'd arrived at the restaurant.

On the way to the Coakley woman's house, with money in hand, Clay marveled at how streamlined the process had become over the last few years: he would withdraw a sum of money, pay a visit to the object of his father's affliction, deliver a well-practiced story about the wisdom of taking the money and dropping out of sight, then whisk away his father for a few days on an impromptu golf, tennis, ski, or sailing trip. Depending on his father's and the girl's reluctance to end the liaison, he might hire a private investigator to uncover the woman's skeletons, then present the damaging information to his father before they returned home. Martin was usually miffed at first, but would eventually agree with Clay that the relationship wouldn't have worked and good-naturedly return to his idle pursuits.

Buying off the gold-diggers revolted Clay, but he had negotiated each of his father's divorce settlements and knew that pre-nuptial agreements were not iron-clad, especially considering his father's tendency to make generous verbal promises in the throes of passion. Even with him handling his father's investments personally, the funds had been rapidly depleted. He could provide handsomely for his father, and the recent settlement check from their drawn out lawsuit would restore Martin's reserves, but Clay was determined to plug the sugar-daddy leak. Consequently, circumventing marriage altogether seemed the most expedient end.

He slowed to scan the road signs. Martin's former girlfriends had lived in slovenly apartments—and worse—so he was surprised to discover this woman owned a relatively nice home in an established neighborhood. Clay wondered if the house was a gift, or maybe an inheritance from the girl's last wealthy boyfriend. He hated to be cynical, but he'd discovered that most of the women who cozied up to his gullible father had a history of rooking older men.

He stopped in front of the sweet-looking white home and smirked. How charming. Unmoved, he parked and made his way up the sidewalk. The top story of his father's home—*his* home really, since he'd assumed the payments and the title—was visible through the top-heavy pine trees. Proximity was a variable he hadn't had to deal with before, but he'd think of something.

Clay filled his lungs with tepid air and climbed the steps heavily, anger toward the unknown woman building with each footfall. *Please don't let her be another stripper.*

He rang the doorbell, then stepped back and prepared himself for the appearance of a garish young woman. Blond and busty, if his father's taste ran true to form. And neither virtue had to be God-given.

When a couple of minutes passed, he rang again, then realized the woman was probably lounging by his father's pool. Just as he turned to leave, a muffled female voice sounded from the other side of the door.

"Can I help you?"

She sounded young—naturally. "Ms. Coakley, I came to talk to you about Martin Castleberry."

Seconds passed, then, "Who are you?"

"I'm Clay Castleberry, his son." He felt like an idiot talking to the door, but apparently the woman inside had no such compunction.

"I didn't know he had a son."

Clay bit the inside of his cheek—he could almost hear the echo in her empty head. How could his father consider marrying the woman and omit the fairly relevant fact that he had a son? Of course, Martin might have told the woman and she'd simply forgotten. If she were that ditzy, at least she'd be a pushover for the money he offered. "Ms. Coakley, we need to talk about the engagement."

"How did you know I was here?"

He shook his head. Great—she was simple *and* paranoid. He floundered for a response that wouldn't spook her. "My father told me."

The handle rattled and the door swung open. "I knew it—he's watching the house through binoculars, isn't he?"

Clay blinked and a bolt of pure male admiration shot through him. Dressed in a short turquoise robe with her dark wet hair falling around her shoulders, Belle Coakley was a vision. Pale hazel eyes flashed from a slender face, flanked by long dark lashes and a surprising display of freckles across the bridge of her small nose. A memory chord pinged, but he couldn't imagine where he might have met the woman. His father's taste in mistresses was definitely improving, but she couldn't be much over twenty-five. A simple, paranoid, *angry* twenty-five.

"Isn't he?" She scowled and took one step forward.

At the flash of thigh, his mind clouded. "Excuse me?"

Her eyes narrowed. "Don't play games with me, mister."

His own ire began to rise, but he didn't want to provoke her further. "I don't know anything about binoculars."

She crossed her arms beneath her breasts. "So, Cliff, what did you want to talk about?"

His neck warmed. "Clay."

Her only acknowledgment was the slight lift of one eyebrow.

In the course of his job to convince venture capitalists to invest in his clients' projects, he'd become a master at interpreting people's expressions, and never had one simple tic infuriated him so. He perused the rigid set of her chin and experienced an uneasy premonition that the woman before him had the potential to unleash more grief than the Castleberry men could handle. The sooner he dispensed with the preliminaries, the better.

"Ms. Coakley, I have a proposition for you."

CHAPTER THREE

ANNABELLE SURVEYED THE IMPOSING MAN who had so effectively dismissed her on the subway. The fact that he didn't even recognize her stiffened her backbone. The cad. No wonder he'd looked familiar—Clay Castleberry resembled his celebrity father in coloring and profile, and, considering his provocative statement, in attitude as well. "A proposition?"

"Perhaps we should step inside."

She hesitated. His arrogant demeanor triggered a row of red warning flags that stretched as far as her mind's eye could see. Still, anything she could find out about the Castleberry family might give her ammunition when reasoning with Belle. Wordlessly, she swept an arm toward the interior of the house, then retreated to allow him to enter. Annabelle pressed her back against the door to avoid contact, but the man's intensity grazed her as tangibly as his arm might have, dredging up an alarming swirl of awareness, which she attributed to too many evenings chatting with her cat.

He had traded the suit for taupe slacks and a long sleeve wheat-colored shirt—expensively cut with a price tag to match, she presumed. He was tall, probably six-two or -three, with powerful shoulders and thighs that strained against his clothing when he moved. She wondered what he did for a living that allowed him to spend enough hours at the gym to maintain that fabulous physique. Tilting her head, she noted the close-clipped hair, the bronzed skin, the confident air—on second thought, Mr. Silver Spoon probably *owned* a gym.

She walked behind him the few paces to the living room and gestured toward the yellow French country couch and chairs. "Have a seat."

He gave the room a quick once-over, then pivoted in the center of the area rug to face her. "I'll stand."

She remained in the doorway, a couple of strides from the front door, which she'd left ajar. Flies be damned—a girl couldn't be too careful with a Castleberry in the vicinity. "Suit yourself."

His gaze traveled the length of her, triggering a ruffled sense of deja vu. She'd taken the time to jam her feet into a pair of her mother's house shoes she stumbled over in the hallway. Admittedly the fur-trimmed white mules were a bit frou-frou, but at least her blue-tipped toes were covered. She knotted the robe tie again for extra security and drew herself up. "Now, what's this all about, Mr. Castleberry?"

He pursed his mouth, as if mulling words, then his face took on the lines of granite. He withdrew a fat white envelope from his front pocket and extended it to her.

Confused, Annabelle took the package. "Is this some kind of dossier?"

"Open it."

She didn't like the tone of his voice, but she slid a short nail under the flap of the envelope. Her heart kicked up at the sight of one hundred dollar bills—lots of them—and she nearly dropped the packet. "What is this?"

"Twenty thousand dollars. Yours, Ms. Coakley, if you walk away from this little charade." He remained unsmiling.

Bewilderment clogged her brain and her throat.

His face gentled for the briefest second. "My father is a sweet, gullible old man who is an easy target for young women who are *charmed* by his nostalgic celebrity." His voice was low and soothing, as if he were speaking to a child. "But believe me, it would be better for all involved if you took this money and disappeared for a few weeks."

She shook her head to clear it.

"Don't be so hasty," he warned. "I'm doing you a favor. After all, what kind of a life would a young woman like you have with a seventy-five-year-old man?"

Annabelle stared until anger and disbelief began to dawn. Surely this man didn't think that she was her mother? She looked at the money in her hand, then back to Clay Castleberry. "You can't be serious."

His gaze bore into her. "Oh, but I am."

"You're offering me twenty thousand dollars?"

He stepped closer, invading her personal space, and his expression turned mocking. "Not enough to make you forget true love?" His voice shifted from silk to sandpaper. He stood so close she could feel the air displacement from his warm breath. "Spare me the fairy tale, Ms. Coakley. My father is the romantic—I don't believe in happy endings."

The man was giving her insight into the kind of family her mother was about to marry into, reinforcing her motivation to rescue Belle. The knowledge that Clay Castleberry had so grossly misinterpreted the situation emboldened her—she had the advantage.

After an appropriate pause, she asked, "And what do you expect in return for the payment?" She conjured up a syrupy smile—fortunately, lawyering required that she master a certain amount of theatrics.

Triumph licked at one corner of his broad unsmiling mouth. "You'll break off the engagement, then leave town for a while."

He stopped, as if allowing her to memorize his orders before proceeding—the man was apparently used to giving commands.

"Then I'll take Martin on a vacation to distract him. When he returns, you'll have changed your phone number and become immune to his attention. Understood?"

Feeling uncharacteristically wicked, Annabelle ran her thumb over the stack of bills. "And if I don't?"

He leaned closer still and placed one hand against the wall over her shoulder. With a half-turn she could have escaped his towering presence, but she remained frozen to the spot. Her breathing became more shallow and she was increasingly aware of her state of near undress. His eyes weren't black after all, but the deepest blue, and framed with enough lines to put him in his early to mid-thirties. His skin emitted a minty aroma—shaving cream, she decided, since his clenched jaw looked newly shorn.

"If you don't," he whispered, his mouth set in a straight line, "I will make things, shall we say, *difficult*?"

She considered her options and decided laughing in his face would be best—and just. Her mouth twitched.

"Twenty-five thousand," he murmured, his voice as sensuous as if he were paying her the grandest of compliments. "And not a penny more."

Even as her fury bloomed, her body responded to his nearness, the traitor. Annabelle wet her lips, perversely driven to provoke the arrogant man. "And what if I told you that I'm devoted to your father?"

For a few seconds, panic drove all other emotion from Clay's chest. This woman exhibited more spunk than the others—was it possible she actually cared for Martin, or was she simply more determined? He searched her face for sincerity, but her intriguing eyes were unreadable. A few strands of walnut-colored hair had dried and fallen forward to frame a face comprised of uncommonly elegant bone structure. Her skin glowed clean and translucent, her cheeks pink, her freckles prominent. The aroma of baby powder invaded his nostrils, reminding him she had recently stepped from the shower and was most likely nude beneath her robe. How many times had his father seen her wearing this robe...and less?

A twinge of envy fluttered in his stomach, but anger chased away the inappropriate feelings as he acknowledged the woman would enjoy knowing she was pushing the buttons of *both* Castleberry men. Struggling to regain control of the situation, his gaze lit upon her mouth, full and rosy. On impulse, he curled his hand around the nape of her neck and dragged her mouth to his. He had no reason to hesitate—his instincts had never led him astray.

Clay registered lush softness and exquisite flavors before she realized he was kissing her. She gasped and stiffened, but he captured her hands and chased her mouth as she tried to wrench away, pressing her shoulders into the wall. She grunted and bit down, but he levered his mouth and stilled her squirming by imprisoning her legs with his, maintaining constant but gentle pressure on her lips.

At last her resistance petered out and she relaxed under his persuasive ministrations. Clay softened the kiss and coaxed her tongue until her mouth moved willingly under his. He had proved his point, but he prolonged the kiss for the sake of sheer accomplishment. When he lifted his head, the sight of her flushed face, disarrayed hair, and swollen mouth fueled his desire. The robe had parted just enough to reveal the swell of her cleavage. His body responded and he very nearly kissed her again. Instead, still leaning into her with their fingers entwined, Clay smirked. "Devoted to my father, did you say?"

Her eyes narrowed. "You're despicable."

For a moment, Clay thought she might spit in his face and the idea amused him. He laughed as he released her and stepped back. The money had fallen to the floor and the bills lay strewn like a forgotten newspaper. She turned her back to straighten her robe, her movements jerky. He scooped up the money, trying not to stare at the slender lines of her calves and ankles, elevated in those ridiculous shoes. Tapping the stack of bills even on a mahogany sideboard, Clay decided the impromptu kiss had been worth the extra five thousand. And he was definitely doing Martin a favor by driving this one away—if their embattled kiss was any indication of the depths of her passion, he had spared his father a certain heart attack during the honeymoon.

"Then we have a deal, Ms. Coakley?"

She still stood with her back to him, her shoulders rising and falling, but at his words, she turned. Anger rolled off her in waves, filling the room. "Take your filthy money and get out."

Clay tamped his irritation, reminding himself of his goal. "Taking advantage of my father's hospitality and generosity might be fun for you at the moment," he said patiently, "but I have news for you, Ms. Coakley. I own the house, the pool and all the other toys you undoubtedly find so intriguing. I also control my father's purse strings. I've dealt with your kind before and I can assure you, you have no place in this family. We don't like outsiders."

Her mouth tightened. "Leave now or I'll call the police."

He ground his teeth, then advanced slowly, making a show of counting the bills. "I was beginning to think you were smarter than the others. Was I wrong?"

She reached for the phone, but he reacted quickly and covered her hand with his own, stilling her movement. Her hand was small and ringless, and her skin felt hot—or was the heat his own? He held up the money with his free hand. "If you don't cooperate, Ms. Coakley, you'll be sorry you ever met me."

Her gaze locked with his and a clock somewhere ticked off several loud seconds. Clay realized he was holding his breath. God, she really was lovely.

"I'm already sorry I met you, Mr. Castleberry. Now get your hand off me."

Her chest rose and fell in a quick rhythm. Her clenched jaw defined her cheekbones and the faint impressions of high dimples. Although he itched to kiss her again, he knew resolve when he saw it, and released her hand. Suddenly tired, Clay shoved the money into his pocket, tempted to let his father drown in his own foolishness this time. Martin hadn't made a responsible decision on his own since Clay's mother had died, and Clay was weary of cleaning up his messes. This woman promised to be a thorn in his side, and he didn't need the hassle. But deep-seated protective feelings for his father compelled him to goad her one last time.

"By the way, I'll be sure to let Martin know just how *devoted* you are to him."

He saw her hand coming, and allowed her to slap him. In fact, he'd expected no less from her. Clay rubbed his stinging jaw.

"Annabelle?"

At the sound of another woman's voice, Clay swung toward the front door. A middle-aged woman stood inside the foyer, her face a mask of surprise, her eyes darting back and forth between him and the woman who'd slapped him.

For a few seconds, no one spoke, then the young robed woman laughed a bit nervously. "Surprise...Mother. I thought we could spend some time together before...you know." Their embrace was a bit abrupt, though they appeared happy to see one another.

Clay's confusion doubled when his father stepped in behind the older woman, his eyes wide and searching. "Clayton? I *thought* that was your car in the driveway. What are you doing here, son?"

He cast about for an appropriately vague answer, his mind spinning. "My, um, business in Paris ended sooner than I expected."

Martin Castleberry frowned. "But what are you doing here, at Belle's?" He placed a hand on the older woman's shoulder, and Clay had the first horrible inkling that something was very wrong. He glanced at the young woman, and her smug look reinforced his suspicion. She angled her chin and adopted an expression of 'We're waiting.'

"Well, I…that is, we—"

"You won't believe it," the young woman cut in, her eyes never leaving his. "Clay and I met accidentally on the train from the airport and he offered to drive me out. Quite a coincidence, huh?"

Clay blinked and a memory surfaced of a slender woman in overalls on the train staring at him. Mentally, he subtracted the yellow sunglasses, freed the bound hair and replaced the baggy clothes with the silky wrap. He couldn't see her blue-tipped toes, but it was the same woman, all right. Dammit, she'd somehow known who he was all along.

The older woman gave the short robe a worried glance, then smiled a bit shakily. "Martin, this is my daughter, Annabelle."

Martin beamed and extended his hand. "What a pleasure. Belle has told me so much about you." He lifted his gaze to Clay, whose limbs felt stiff with impending doom. "Clay, I want you to meet the most important woman in my life." He gave the older woman's shoulder a squeeze. "This is Belle Coakley, my fiancée."

Clay's lips moved and he forced some inane pleasantry through his teeth. Meanwhile, his heart raced and heat flooded his face. Annabelle Coakley looked as if she were enjoying his torment immensely. Clay set his jaw, which still tingled from her slap. He'd mistaken the woman's daughter for the bride-to-be, and the little phony had played along. What kind of trick did she have up her sleeve? Did she think she could extort even more than he'd offered?

Belle clapped her hands. "Oh, isn't this the most wonderful turn of events? Annabelle is here early and Clayton has come home. The two of you can help us plan the ceremony, and—" she dimpled, "—we can all get to know each other." She gave Annabelle another hug, this one affording Clay a generous view of the back of Annabelle's toned thighs. He averted his gaze and gave his father a tight smile.

Martin crossed to him and clapped him on the back. “Our marriage was going to be a surprise, son, but I couldn’t be happier to have you here.” He lowered his voice to a whisper. “This is the one, Clay. Just look at her, isn’t she something?”

Clay stared at the two women standing arm in arm, but his attention kept straying to the dark-haired beauty who had duped him. Annabelle wore an expression of veiled loathing. “She’s something, all right.”

“Is that a one hundred dollar bill?” Belle asked, stooping to pick up a bill lying on the foyer tile.

Clay’s stomach flipped over, and the wad of cash in his pocket burned his thigh.

“Oh, that’s mine,” Annabelle said. “I must have dropped it. I…don’t have a pocket,” she said, gesturing to her robe as if she made perfect sense. “In fact—” She beamed. “—lunch is on me.”

Clay looked to the ceiling—how magnanimous of her.

“Great,” Martin said in a happy, booming voice. “Let’s order take-out and have lunch around the pool. I can’t think of a better way to catch up on everyone’s life.” His father grinned. “I’m so glad you kids are already acquainted. How serendipitous for you to meet! It *must* be a good omen. We’ll be seeing a lot of each other in the future—holidays, maybe even family vacations.”

Clay scowled.

“Just think,” Belle said, her bubbly mood matching his father’s as she squeezed Annabelle tighter, “none of us have to be alone any longer—we’ll be one big, happy family.”

But one look at Annabelle Coakley’s narrowed eyes and kiss-bruised mouth and Clay felt decidedly *un*happy.

CHAPTER FOUR

"MOM," ANNABELLE SAID, holding up a bright pink teeny-weeny bikini. "I don't think this is a good idea."

Belle pursed her lips and nodded. "You're right—the pink will wash you out. Try the green suit, dear." Then her mother turned back to the vanity mirror to pat her hair, which had, since Annabelle's last visit, transformed from salt and pepper gray to a shade that fell somewhere between butter and Parkay margarine.

Annabelle rehung the barely-there suit in the closet of the Castleberry changing house and drew a deep breath for patience. "I meant spending the afternoon with the Castleberrys isn't a good idea." A strip of aqua colored pool water winked at her through a shuttered window. The otherwise soothing sight rankled her, as did the familiarity with which her mother moved about this man's property, and even the posh amenities in the changing cottage. Leather furniture, pale textured wallpaper, real artwork, terra cotta tiled floors—the place was nicer than the *home* she was agonizing over buying. "How about just you and I zip down to Buckhead for lunch?"

Disappointment flashed in Belle's bright blue eyes. Her pale brows were finely arched and wonder of wonders, she wore eyeliner—violet-colored, no less. "Oh, but Martin does so want to get to know you better, and I just know you're going to love him, too. You and I can go downtown tomorrow when we'll have the entire day to enjoy each other's company." She stood and walked toward Annabelle. Her mother's figure had undergone some drastic changes, too—a result of her new kickboxing classes, no doubt.

Annabelle tried not to wince at the sight of the diamond solitaire on her mother's ring finger as Belle grasped her hands. "Sweetheart, this might be my only chance to interact with Clayton before he returns to Paris. Then you and I will spend every moment of the week before the wedding together." She surveyed Annabelle's overalls with a worried smile. "Perhaps we can look for you some clothes tomorrow."

Annabelle smiled—*here* was the mother she remembered. "Hopefully the airline will find my luggage by tomorrow."

Belle reached up and freed Annabelle's hair from its clip. "He's rather attractive, don't you think?"

She frowned. "Who?"

"Clayton."

Her frown deepened. "I didn't notice." *I was too busy counting his bribe and fighting off his advances.*

"He reminds me of the way Martin looked in *Streetwise.*" Her mother adopted a faraway expression. "Martin was so dashing—I must have seen that movie a dozen times when it premiered."

"Wasn't he a philandering con-man in that movie?" *Well, okay, maybe I didn't exactly fight the man off, but I certainly didn't enjoy that kiss.*

"He redeemed himself in the end." Belle sighed. "Life is a bit astonishing, isn't it? Imagine, me marrying a movie star."

The beginnings of a headache needled Annabelle's temple. Her mother seemed almost giddy. Granted, the grandeur of Martin's house—or rather, his *son's* house if Clay was telling the truth—was impressive, but surely her mother wasn't flattered to the point of blindness. "Has Mr. Movie Star asked you to sign a prenuptial agreement?"

Belle's brightly-colored mouth turned down. "No. I offered, but he refused." She turned to flip through the handful of colorful swimsuits hanging in the closet, then removed a sleek green one-piece and held it up to Annabelle. "Try this one."

"Mom," Annabelle said carefully, "what kind of man maintains a closet full of women's bathing suits?"

Belle simply laughed. "Don't hold it against him, dear. He's used to a great deal of female attention."

She stared at her mother, then wet her lips. "I see. And do you expect this behavior to continue after the marriage?"

Her mother shrugged. "It's really none of my business."

This was the same woman who advised her to drop Billy Hardigan in sixth grade because he gave a Valentine to Jill Normandy?

"Don't look so surprised, dear. He's a grown man, and I've become more liberal in my middle age."

She gulped air, wanting to jam her fingers into her ears to block her mother's words. "Mom, we need to talk—"

"Please, darling." Belle held up one hand. "Let's spend the afternoon relaxing by the pool, and tonight we'll have a nice, long talk, okay?"

One look into Belle's velvety eyes and Annabelle crumbled. Her mother had never asked anything of her in her life. Besides, she wasn't looking forward to the disagreement she was sure would result from their 'talk.' And she didn't want to be accused of not giving Martin a chance. Remembering her earlier vow to respond with reserved enthusiasm, she nodded. "Just for you."

Her mother beamed and kissed her cheek. "Thank you, sweetheart. I'll fix us some iced tea and meet you poolside."

Annabelle watched her mother slip through the door and squelched the childish urge to run after her and hug her around the knees. Fighting sudden and panicky tears, she dropped to the soft creme-colored chaise, and covered her face with her hands. For the first time she realized how much her mother had probably worried about her over the years. Was there anything worse than watching someone you love make a huge mistake? A lesson learned, she thought ruefully—caring about a person led to inevitable anguish.

After a few moments, she inhaled deeply and lifted her head. Sitting here feeling sorry for herself wasn't helping to fulfill her promise to her father. She slowly disrobed and pulled on the green bathing suit after inspecting it carefully. Adjusting straps and rearranging extra fabric, she noted wryly that Martin was obviously used to entertaining busty women. Having spent countless hours of her youth in full-coverage regulation swimwear, she felt naked in the high- and low-cut shiny emerald suit that seemed more suitable for posing than for swimming. How could her mother overlook Martin's tendencies? Did she honestly think the man had changed?

Her mind raced like a treadmill, spinning the circumstances in hopes that some solution would fall out of the mess. She hadn't counted on Clay Castleberry's presence, and although he too seemed intent on preventing their parents' marriage, she resented his inference that she or her mother was the kind of woman who could be bought off. She half-smiled at the case of mistaken identity, but the memory of his insistent kiss rose up to remind her the joke had been on her. No man had dared to kiss her with such authority, and her wilting response had shocked her. The playboy had simply taken her by surprise, she reasoned. Now that she knew what kind of man she was dealing with, she would be on guard.

She hadn't yet divulged to her mother his attempt to pay her off. To dissuade her mother from this marriage, she needed something on the senior Castleberry, not the son.

The son.

Annabelle pursed her mouth in irritation. The man upset her equilibrium, and her instincts told her to sit on the incident for now in the event she needed leverage against him later. Just a few minutes in his company reinforced her belief that most men and women in this day and age were better adapted for single life—especially the Castleberry men and the Coakley women. In her opinion, the institution of marriage had been diminished to the level of a feast for those who were gluttons for punishment.

Annabelle tugged at the skinny bottom of the swimsuit and frowned. She wasn't about to allow her mother be taken in by a smooth-talking womanizer, and Clay Castleberry's meddling would only complicate matters. She ground her teeth in frustration—if only she could snap her fingers and make the infuriating man disappear.

Along with the memory of his pilfered kiss.

Clay brushed his fingers against the slick painted wall of the pool, then tucked into a somersault. With a leisurely but powerful kick, he pushed off to swim back to the shallow end, enjoying the mindless roar of the water rushing past his ears and the stretch of his shoulder muscles. When he reached the opposite wall, he slung the water from his eyes and leaned his head back.

The sky reigned clear and blue, the afternoon temperature had climbed to the mid-eighties, and a southerly breeze stirred the needles of the soaring pines bordering the house. A perfect day...and a perfect mess.

Annabelle Coakley had arrived to ensure her mother milked his father for as much money as possible, and he had obliged by extending an offer as soon as she landed. The only thing worse than a gold digger, was a gold digger who had a divorce attorney for a daughter.

The sound of a sliding glass door opening captured his attention, and the object of his consternation stepped out, curvy and leggy and unaware she was being observed. Feeling stubbornly entitled after the way she'd duped him, he regarded every inch of her lithe figure and the way she moved. Her dark hair hung loose past her shoulders, thick and straight. The woman was a beauty, but seemed a bit self-conscious. She pulled at the leg openings of a vaguely familiar bathing suit in a futile attempt to cover more skin, giving him choking glimpses of private areas beneath. The pool water wasn't cool enough by far to stifle his body's natural response.

Her eyes were shielded by yellow-lensed sunglasses, but she lifted her face toward the sun. His father had said she now lived in Michigan, so she probably appreciated the warm weather. She lifted her arms overhead and stretched tall, rising on the balls on her feet and arching her back. Her breasts rode high and her stomach went concave, emphasizing the hills and valleys of her toned body. Unadulterated appreciation pumped through his loins. At another time, in another place, he might have entertained the idea of enticing her into his bed, but this woman represented more complications than a dozen of the start-up ventures he'd organized.

She turned and scanned the patio and landscaping—sizing up their worth, no doubt. When her gaze landed on him relaxing silently in the water, she stiffened.

He inclined his head in acknowledgment.

"You might have let me know you were here." Her accusing voice carried across the water.

"Funny," he said, squinting up at her. "I thought *you* were the guest. I sort of own this place."

She walked to the edge of the pool and crossed her arms. "That's the strangest apology I ever heard."

Clay lifted one eyebrow. "Apology?"

Her smile was deceptively sweet. "Does senility run in your family? An apology for *in*sulting and *a*ssaulting me."

He lifted the other eyebrow. "You've never been kissed?"

Emotions played over her face, ending in fury, which added a pleasing color to her cheeks. "Yes. But not against my will and with brute force."

"Brute force?" He laughed. "Drop the debutante act, counselor. You weren't rushing to clear up the misunderstanding."

She looked around as if to assess how she might dispose of his body if she drowned him, then glared. "With your disposition, you must work with machines."

"Venture capitalists."

Her mouth quirked to one side. "Same thing. You don't have anything to say for your earlier behavior?"

To keep from focusing on her legs, which, at his angle, seemed to go on for days, Clay closed his eyes and leaned his head back. "Yes. You're overreacting."

She was silent for so long, he was tempted to look again, but didn't. Not that he needed to since her silhouette was branded on his mind. Finally she spoke.

"Mr. Castleberry, aren't you afraid I'll say something to your father or my mother about your little bribe?"

Without the distraction of looking at her, he detected the remnants of a southern accent when she pronounced his name. She was being formal, was she? He smiled, eyes still closed. "Ms. Coakley, if I know my father, he's probably *expecting* me to help him get off the hook, and I suspect you've already spoken to your mother." He rolled stiff shoulders and exhaled when a pain shot through his neck—a fitting ailment for the moment, he acknowledged. "That said, I assure you, twenty-five thousand is my final offer."

A terrific splash preceded the wave that washed over his face. Clayton swallowed a mouthful of chlorinated water, but managed to keep it out of his lungs. When his vision cleared, he watched her swim away from him, her overhand crawl flawless, her kicks perfectly executed, her direction arrow-straight.

When she reached the other side, she bobbed to the surface and leaned back, directly opposite him. Her expression was one of pure irreverence. With her dark hair slicked back from her face, her sculpted features stood out in relief, her eyebrows, dark wings above golden eyes. God, she was glorious-looking. Thirty feet of azure water separated them, but his senses were as rapt as if her body were wedged against his.

"Since you're a venture capitalist," she said, just loud enough to carry to his buzzing ears, "you know where you can *venture* to put your twenty-five thousand."

Clay clenched his jaw. He hadn't learned to negotiate multi-million dollar deals by wearing his emotions on his sleeve. Time for a different tack. He flashed his most charming smile. "You're an excellent swimmer."

She shrugged, the movement emphasizing her toned upper arms. "Swimming meant the difference between a good college and a great one. And it helps to unclutter my mind—I like the discipline."

Shrewd, resourceful…dangerous. "From your mother's reaction earlier, I assume your visit was unexpected." Perhaps she'd arrived to ensure the Coakley's future stake in the Castleberry fortune without her mother's knowledge…or perhaps her mother was simply a good actress.

"From your father's reaction, I assume the same thing about your visit."

No answer—just as he expected. He floated away from the wall, in no particular direction. "I felt compelled to return. My father has a history of making bad decisions."

She moved her arms back and forth to propel herself in lazy circles, but her voice sliced the air razor sharp. "That's strange—my mother started making bad decisions only after she met your father."

"Am I supposed to believe that you're against this marriage?"

"You may believe what you want, Mr. Castleberry."

He glanced at her over his shoulder. "Are you this evasive in the courtroom?"

Her little square chin raised a notch. "Yes, I'm against this marriage. My mother is a decent, trusting woman, and I don't want to see her taken advantage of."

She had drawn close enough for him to see the light freckles across her nose, and her delicate ears. He searched her face for signs of duplicity. Was she simply setting him up—again? "My father is also very trusting, and I don't want to see *him* taken advantage of."

Her laugh was quick and dry. She swam closer, leaning forward. "But your father is the one who has a reputation for jumping from marriage to marriage—philandering is practically synonymous with the name Castleberry."

Her words burned a trail to the pit of his stomach. *Casanova Castleberry.* He'd always hated the nickname the trade rags had given to his father. While the whole snickering world had placed bets on how long his father's current relationship would last, Clay had been relegated to the care of house staff, and rarely saw his father. He resented her casual reference to a subject that had so affected his childhood.

"And for all I know," he said quietly, "the Coakley women could have a reputation for attaching themselves to wealthy men."

Her scoff seemed convincing. "My father wasn't exactly a wealthy man, Mr. Castleberry."

"But well-off?"

Annabelle frowned. "We were comfortable."

They now floated only a few feet from each other in the water. Her legs were slim columns, the blue polish on her toes, splotches of bright drifting color. "So maybe your mother wants to be more than comfortable."

Her eyes blazed. "My mother is the most unselfish person I've ever known."

"Really? I noticed she chose a good-sized rock for an engagement ring."

They circled, like wary animals, treading water. "She didn't choose that garish ring, your father gave it to her."

"She didn't turn it down." If his father's financial future wasn't at stake, he might have enjoyed their banter.

"My mother is much too gracious. Why else would she put up with a man who keeps spare bathing suits for his water bunnies?"

Clay wanted to laugh at the indignant look on her face, but he was confused. "What are you talking about?"

"This misshapen garment," she said, plucking at the strap of the green suit she wore. "From the closet of your father's changing cottage. Who knows who wore it last?"

A smile curved his lips as he realized the source of her outrage.

"Did I miss the punch line?" she demanded.

"Valerie."

"Excuse me?"

"I believe Valerie wore that, um, *misshapen* suit last."

She looked triumphant. "One of your father's girlfriends, no doubt—heavy emphasis on 'girl.'"

He heard the sliding glass door open just as he shook his head and grinned. "No. One of mine, heavy emphasis on—" He nodded toward the sagging suit top, "—shall we say 'heavy'?"

Her mouth tightened into a pink bow and she looked down at the suit as if she might tear it off on the spot.

"Go ahead, I wouldn't mind," he whispered, intimating he could read her thoughts. Water droplets laced her eyelashes like crystals. Then he nodded toward their parents who carried food-laden trays. "But it might give them the wrong idea."

She sputtered a scalding comment to his back as he swam to the edge and pushed himself up and out of the water. Luckily, his towel lay across a nearby chair so he could cover the effect she was having on his body. He'd been without female company too long—maybe he would give Valerie a call. Of course, the blonde might be engaged or married by now for all he knew. He remembered inviting her to stay at the house for a week last spring while his father vacationed and he house-sat, but he didn't realize she'd left behind her swimming wardrobe. And he didn't remember her looking as sexy in the green suit as Annabelle Coakley.

He greeted Martin and Belle and accepted a glass of unsweetened iced tea. Out of the corner of his eye, he watched the young woman in the pool swim laps with unerring precision. Every smooth kick defined lean hamstrings and nicely curved hips. Her hair floated behind her like a dark silky flag.

Belle was talking to his father in the background. When she mentioned Annabelle's name, he honed in on her words.

"...so proud of her...she's buying a house...between her law school loans and her dreadful state salary, I can't imagine how she was able to save thirty thousand dollars...maybe Mike is splitting the cost with her..."

Clay glanced back to the woman slicing through the water like a mermaid. She moved well, conjuring up thoughts of limber positions. He set his jaw against the answering pulse of desire in his midsection.

So Annabelle Coakley had secrets, did she? He knew the concerned-daughter act was too good to be true—she was up to something. After excusing himself, he walked into the house, pulled out his cell phone, and punched in a number from memory.

While the phone rang, he couldn't decipher the tickle at his conscience that he hoped he was wrong this time. But he always trusted his instincts, and right now they shouted that the young Miss Coakley was the most hazardous person he'd encountered in some time.

And who the devil was Mike?

When the person on the other end answered, Clay spoke in a low tone. "Henry, this is Clayton Castleberry. I need a background check, basic stuff for now. The name is Belle Coakley." He spelled his father's fiancée's name, her street address, and approximated her age. "I have another name for you, Henry, but I'll need the works on this one, plus local surveillance. Ready? A-N-N-A ..."

CHAPTER FIVE

"HOW'S IT GOING?" Michaela asked.

Annabelle glanced across the crowded court of the upscale mall to where her mother stood waiting for her. Belle looked small and soft and vulnerable—God, how she loved her. Annabelle swallowed and spoke into her cell phone. "Not so well, Mike."

"Your mother hasn't been receptive to your advice?"

"I, um, actually haven't had the chance to speak to her much about the wedding. She wasn't home when I first arrived, and when she came home, Melvin was with her."

"I thought his name was Martin."

"Whatever. Anyway, she wanted to spend the afternoon by his pool so she could get to know his son—"

"Heeeeey, a son?"

Annabelle frowned. "Don't get excited, Mike. He's a Castleberry through and through—rude, arrogant, pushy—"

"How old?"

"I don't know, mid-thirties, I guess."

"Good-looking?"

"No." She hesitated as Clay's blue eyes rose in her mind. "Well...maybe in a dark and brooding kind of way, but that type went out with *Wuthering Heights*."

"What's his name? Is he rich? Is he single?"

She sighed. "Clayton Castleberry, probably, and I couldn't care less."

"Gee, since you're there, Annabelle, you might as well—"

"Mike!"

"Sorry. What were you saying?"

"Well, after I spent an afternoon by the pool watching Mother and Melvin—"

"Martin."

"—fawn all over each other—" she rubbed her sunburned nose which had become even more populated with freckles, "—she and I went home to have a nice, long talk."

"And?"

"And she'd drunk three glasses of wine by the pool, so she fell asleep before she could change into her pajamas. *My* mother—the woman who used to think cooking with sherry was naughty."

"So what did *you* do all evening?" Mike asked in a sing-songy voice.

"Worked on my laptop," she answered in a similar tone. Actually, she'd sat with her hands on the keyboard and sent hateful vibes to Clay Castleberry, wherever he was, for the way he'd treated her. The man threw her off balance, made her feel as if she were always in response mode. "Anyway, mother and I are getting ready to have lunch, and I hope to talk some sense into her."

"Go easy, Annabelle."

"One day she'll thank me."

"Good grief, you sound like a mother yourself."

"Bite your tongue. How's everything at the office?"

"Fine. Your real estate agent called—her e-mail is broken."

Annabelle smiled. Mike was an able paralegal, but she wasn't exactly computer savvy. "Does she have a date for closing on the house?"

"Thursday of the week you return. And she's faxing a form you need to fill out listing the source of your down payment—she said the bank needs it for their records."

Annabelle frowned and chewed on her lower lip. "Okay, um, sure. Can you scan in the form and e-mail it to me?"

"You're asking *me*?"

"Mike, you have to join the rest of the world sooner or later."

"Later is good."

"I'll be looking for a note *and* the attachment. Have Mitch in the systems department show you how to use the scanner—he has a crush on you anyway."

"Oh, great. You have a handsome, rich, single, son of a celebrity on the line, and I have Mitch and his pocket protector."

"I don't—" Annabelle stopped, refusing to be lured into a response that might be misinterpreted, although her blood pressure was definitely escalating. "How is everything else at the office?"

"Quiet, actually. I've been taking advantage of the time to call around about apartments. My rent just increased by half, and I have thirty days to find a new place."

"My apartment will be up for grabs soon."

"Yeah, but it's too far away from the university. By the way, I stopped by to pick up your mail and change Shoakie's litter box."

"Did the little princess show herself?"

"She hissed at me from the top of the bookcase. I felt honored."

Annabelle laughed. "Thanks for checking on her. I have to run."

"Try to be nice around the young Mr. Castleberry, and please don't let him see you in your overalls."

She looked down at her sole outfit and frowned. "Bye, Mike." After hanging up, Annabelle threaded her way through the crowd back to her mother. Belle, looking smart in a white pantsuit, smiled wide. "Our table is ready, dear."

The hostess of the little bistro gave Annabelle's overalls a quick once-over, then led them to a tiny table set with a pale yellow tablecloth and fresh flowers. The brunch menus were hand printed on thick greenish paper textured with seeds and leaves.

"This restaurant is one of my and Martin's favorite places to eat," her mother gushed.

"All roads lead back to Martin," Annabelle mumbled under her breath.

"Hmm?"

"I asked what do you and Martin usually order?"

Her mother rattled off a list of elegant dishes. Annabelle stared and tried to listen, but she kept fading out, picturing the times when her mother sat across from her at the elbow-worn family dinner table, sifting through recipes to create a Fourth of July or Thanksgiving feast. The consummate homemaker and matriarch, Belle Coakley's life revolved around her husband, her daughter, and her neighborhood. To Annabelle's knowledge, her mother had never set foot in this mall—she said the atmosphere was much too pricey and snobbish, preferring suburban discount stores and clearance sales.

Now she wore department store makeup and designer jeans—*jeans*, for heaven's sake—and seemed impossibly happy. Hurt stabbed at Annabelle. If her mother was happy with all the trappings Martin Castleberry could provide, had Belle been unhappy while living with her father?

"Annabelle?"

She blinked her mother's worried face into focus.

"Are you feeling all right, dear?"

"N-never better."

"Is everything all right at your office?"

"Hm? Oh, yes, Mike said things were actually quiet. She's keeping an eye on Shoakie for me, too."

"Such a nice girl." Her mother lifted her shoulders in an exaggerated shrug. "I can't understand why neither of you beautiful young women has been snapped up by a husband."

"Mom—"

"Speaking of which, I have something for you, dear."

Annabelle watched her mother rummage in a huge black tote, half afraid she would whip out a six foot accountant. Instead Belle withdrew a small black velvet jeweler's box with a silver bow and handed it to her.

"What's this?"

"Open it."

Baffled, she removed the bow and opened the lid of the hinged box. A familiar small square diamond in a white gold setting winked back at her, and a lump immediately lodged in her throat. "Your engagement ring?"

Belle nodded. "I want you to have it, and I know your father would be pleased."

Blinking rapidly, she shook her head. "But Daddy gave you this ring—"

Her mother shushed her. "It was going to be yours someday anyway, and this way you'll have it to enjoy for many years. Try it on."

With shaking hands, she slipped it onto her left ring finger, honored to wear the symbol of her parents' matrimonial promise, but troubled to see it leave her mother's hand. "It's a little big," she murmured, turning the ring freely.

"We'll have it sized," her mother said, nodding with approval. "It's beautiful against your long fingers. And there's still plenty of room for other rings," she added with a wink.

Annabelle swallowed, but the lump remained. "Thank you."

Her mother clasped her hand. "You're welcome."

She stared at her mother's hand and a question she'd pondered yesterday resurfaced. "Where's your…?" A flush warmed her cheeks and she let the question die on her lips when she realized she might not want to hear the answer.

"My wedding ring?" Belle filled in. "I took it off," she said, pulling her new engagement ring up to her knuckle to reveal a dip in her flesh made from wearing a band for thirty-some years. A warm smile played over her mouth. "But it will always be close to my heart."

Hurt plowed through Annabelle's chest, leaving a wide, raw furrow. Protest hovered on her tongue. *No, don't divest yourself of Daddy's things…don't forget the life you had with him…don't forget who you are.* Instead she simply stared at an unfamiliar, sophisticated version of her mother and wondered how much more of her she would lose before this situation ended.

A waitress came by to deliver fresh-squeezed orange juice and to take their orders, bridging the bittersweet moment. While her mother communicated her somewhat complex order—she was counting her fat grams—Annabelle slipped off the ring and tucked the box safely into her purse.

"So," she said when they were alone, forcing cheer into her voice and lifting her glass. "What's on the agenda for the rest of the day?"

"I was hoping you'd help me choose a wedding gown."

She swallowed hard and the tart citrus burned her throat. "A wedding gown?"

"And your dress, too, of course. I was thinking a mother-daughter combination, you know, like when you were little?"

Seizing the opening, Annabelle wiped her mouth, then spoke carefully. "Mom, don't you think you're rushing into this wedding just a tad?"

Her mother dimpled. "Probably, but that doesn't make it wrong."

"You once told me that few good decisions are made quickly. Why are you in such a hurry to be married?"

Belle blushed and glanced down at her folded hands. "Why are most couples in a hurry to marry?"

She translated her mother's expression, then gripped the edges of the table. "Oh my God, you're pregnant." Her mother was in her fifties, but hadn't a woman in her sixties given birth not too long ago? Her mind swirled with the medical implications, and perspiration warmed her hairline.

Belle's face crinkled in laughter. "No, dear, I'm not pregnant." She leaned forward slightly and lowered her voice. "In my day, a man and woman were eager to marry so they could become intimate."

At that moment, Annabelle not only wished she hadn't broached the subject, but she also regretted having made the trip to Atlanta. Mortification washed over her and her tongue felt gluey. "You're going to marry Melvin Castleberry so you can *sleep* with him?"

"It's 'Martin,' dear, and I want to marry him because I adore him." Her mother hesitated, then added, "And yes, I have to admit the strain of resisting one another physically is becoming somewhat unbearable."

Annabelle rested her elbows on the table and pressed fingers to her temples. Her trained mind sifted through the options and came up with two: She could either encourage her mother to set aside her moral beliefs and have premarital sex with this playboy in the hopes she would get him out of her system, or she could stand by and watch her mother marry him for all the wrong reasons. *I-yie-yie*, what a choice.

"I didn't mean to embarrass you," her mother murmured. "I assumed you were no longer a virgin, what with college orgies and all."

Annabelle peeked at her mother through her fingers. "Mom, what on earth are you talking about?"

"Sex, dear."

"I know, but I've never—" She frowned, flustered. "This is not about *my* sex life!"

The three women at the nearest table cast curious glances in their direction. Annabelle glared back until they feigned interest in the menu, then she heaved a deep breath. Where had she left off? Oh yeah—the impossible decision. She took another sip of her juice, then began again, calmer now. "Mom, I admire your um, abstinence, but surely you realize that physical attraction is not enough reason to say 'I do.'"

Belle nodded. "I agree that a good marriage can't be based on sex, but it's impossible to have a good marriage *without* good sex."

I can't believe we're having this conversation, I can't believe we're having this conversation. Annabelle reached into her purse and pulled out a folded newspaper page. Clearing her throat, she flattened the creases against the smooth tabletop. "Have you seen this article printed in the entertainment section of *America's News* a few months ago?"

Belle frowned. "No."

Annabelle pushed the paper across the table. The headline read 'Casanova Castleberry Cashes in on Claim,' and the article was surrounded by photos of Martin Castleberry with some of his former starlet girlfriends.

Her mother dismissed the piece with a wave. "The studio Martin made movies for finally agreed to pay him the money he earned, and the papers are making a big deal out of it. Frankly, they *should* expose those producers who tried to steal from him."

Annabelle pressed her lips together, then said, "The only person exposed in this article is Martin Castleberry. The reporter spent ten words describing his settlement with the production company, and ten paragraphs describing his penchant for young women."

"Martin is different now."

"Leopards don't change their spots, Mom."

"He loves me," Belle insisted.

She clasped her mother's hand. "I don't want to see you get hurt. Maybe Martin does love you, for now. But as soon as the novelty of your romance wears thin, he'll be looking for...more excitement. That's how men like Martin and Clay Castleberry operate."

Her mother angled her head. "Clay? What does Clayton have to do with this?"

A flush tickled her neck, and she averted her eyes from her mother's perceptive scrutiny. "Nothing. Other than it's easy to see the man is following in his father's wayward footsteps."

"You're still upset about the bathing suit?" Belle smiled. "I told you, Clay is accustomed to lots of female attention."

"I thought you were referring to Melvin."

"*Martin*, dear. And maybe he was a bit restless in the past, but now my Martin is a one-woman man. Clay, on the other hand, is a very eligible bachelor."

Annabelle bristled because his name resurrected thoughts of his baited bantering. "Bachelor, yes. But 'eligible' implies that a person is someone others would find desirable." She swallowed. Had she actually said 'desirable'? "And desirable isn't a word I would attribute to Clay...I mean, to Clayton... Castleberry."

Her mother quirked an eyebrow, but before she could speak, Annabelle tapped her finger on the article. "Don't change the subject. I don't want to pick up the paper a few months from now and see you listed as a—" She consulted the article. "A 'Castleberry cast-off.'"

Her mother seemed infuriatingly unmoved. "Really, Annabelle, I appreciate your concern, but you're worrying for no reason."

"Worrying for no reason?"

A man being seated at a table behind her mother jerked his head around at her raised voice. Her mother looked disapproving.

Annabelle puffed out her cheeks with an expelled breath. "I'm sorry, Mom, but I have more objectivity about this marriage than you do, and I worry because I love you."

Belle squeezed her hand. "You need to get a hobby, dear."

Shocked into silence, Annabelle simply stared. When she recovered, she struggled to keep her temper at bay. "What?"

"A hobby. You know—line-dancing, photography, origami—something to occupy your time."

She poked her tongue into her cheek, then said, "Typically, my seventy-hours-a-week job keeps me pretty occupied."

"I mean something fun. Do you have a manfriend?"

"If you mean a boyfriend—"

"Don't waste time on the boys, love, you need a man, a worthy partner."

"Mom, I don't have the time or the inclination—"

"Ah, here's our food," Belle exclaimed. The waitress lowered their plates to the table, and Annabelle stared miserably at her Belgium waffle sprinkled with pecans. Her mother lifted a bite of fruit quiche into her mouth and closed her eyes in appreciation. When Annabelle remained frozen, her mother looked at her watch. "I hate to hurry you, dear, but I know you need to shop for a few things, and they're expecting us at the bridal boutique at two."

Exasperated and exhausted, Annabelle simply nodded, unreasonably disturbed by her mother's words. A manfriend? She squashed the sudden image of Clay Castleberry's mocking face. Her hunger, she decided, was making her light-headed. They would eat, and she would try to get through to her mother again later.

She sighed. "Pass the syrup, please."

"Dad, how much do you really know about this Coakley woman?" Clay slowed his jogging pace so his father could converse without becoming winded in the mid-morning heat, although Martin's physical condition never failed to impress him.

Martin cocked one silver eyebrow. "What are you getting at, Clay?"

"Come on, Dad, we've been through this before. Don't tell me the thought that she's interested in getting her hands on your settlement hasn't crossed your mind."

"I most certainly will tell you that, because it hasn't."

"Well, it crossed mine."

Martin scoffed. "Obviously. Son, you're too young to be so cynical."

Clay bit the inside of his cheek. "And you're too old to be so naïve."

His father jogged a few more steps before saying, "Belle Coakley doesn't have a manipulative thought in her head."

With much effort, Clay resisted the urge to comment about the absence of other thoughts in the woman's head. Actually, she did seem nice, but so did most of them, in the beginning. Besides, he was now less concerned about Belle Coakley than her cohort. "What about the manipulative thoughts in the head of her daughter?"

His father glanced at him sideways. "Annabelle? She seems like a nice enough girl, Clay. Kind of fetching, too, don't you think?"

Clay stumbled, then regained his footing. "Don't tell me you've decided to trade in the mother for the daughter." Chagrin slashed through him every time he thought of mistaking Annabelle for his father's fiancée.

Martin laughed, breaking stride long enough to clap Clay on the back. "Of course not. Belle is the woman for me. I was thinking of you, son. I thought I noticed a certain spark between the two of you."

A dry laugh escaped him, and he inadvertently lengthened his stride. "That spark was from the girl's white-hot poker tongue. And I don't trust her."

"That slip of a woman? What's to be scared about?"

Clay frowned. "I said I don't *trust* her."

"Same thing, if a woman's involved. A woman you like, that is."

He stumbled again—damned new running shoes. "Your eyesight must be going, Dad. I certainly don't like the woman."

"No, still twenty-twenty," Martin said, and laughed again. "It seems I am cursed with perfect physical health."

It's your mental health that worries me.

"She takes after Belle," his father continued. "Quite a looker."

Prima donna.

"And demure."

Stuck up.

"And she's an attorney, so she must be intelligent."

Or conniving. "Dad, have you broached the subject of a prenuptial agreement?"

"For your information, Belle offered, and I turned her down."

"Dad—"

"Clay," his father cut in. "I want to grow old with Belle, and I don't intend to curse our union by preparing for its end before we even take our vows."

They reached the end of the running track and slowed. Clay pretended to concede with a conciliatory nod, but his father's words erased the last doubt about the task before him: If Martin wouldn't even insist on a prenuptial agreement, then he had no choice but to put a stop to the wedding.

His father put his hands on his hips to catch his breath. "Belle and I couldn't be happier that you two kids are going to stand up with us at the ceremony." Suddenly his eyes warmed. "Clay, I can't tell you what it means to me that you cut your trip short to be here for the wedding."

Protective feelings welled in his chest, followed quickly by guilt, which persisted more stubbornly than doubt. "No problem, Dad." He funneled all his black emotion toward the Coakley women in general, and toward Annabelle Coakley in particular. Since his childhood, women had been the source of all the Castleberry family problems. Seductresses. Spendthrifts. Mischief-makers. Who needed them? He nodded toward the running path. "I think I'll take another turn."

"Sure thing, son, I'll see you later. Remember—we're due to be fitted for our tuxedoes at two."

Clay wanted to object, but as long as the day's plans didn't include the presence of the Coakley women, he'd humor his father. "Two. Right." Then he took off, digging in for a final lap, determined to outrun the troublesome thoughts of a certain leggy, mouthy brunette.

CHAPTER SIX

ANNABELLE SHIVERED—bridal boutiques gave her the heebie jeebies. The notion of a store devoted entirely to the task of making a woman look good enough for her wedding day grated on her nerves. Especially since she'd known too many clients who'd later hocked those pricey gowns in order to have enough money to file for divorce.

Out of the corner of her eye, a sleeveless white floor-length crepe gown encased in a glass box the size of a phone booth captured her attention. She paused to examine the sleek lines and pursed her lips in begrudged admiration.

On the other hand, if she *did* by some *remote* miracle *ever* entertain even the *thought* of taking a *chance* on walking down the aisle *someday* in the *very* distant future, well, then this little frock wasn't half bad.

"Do you like the pink one, dear?"

She whirled guiltily to inspect her mother's choice. The color was a bit garish, but just as she had with the last twenty-seven dresses, Annabelle smiled and nodded. "It's lovely."

Belle's brow wrinkled. "They're all lovely, I'm afraid. I simply can't decide."

Growing weary, Annabelle sighed. "It really doesn't matter—" She broke off at her mother's hurt expression, then cast about for mending words. "It doesn't matter which one you choose, because you'll look beautiful, regardless."

Her mother beamed, then turned when a salesclerk emerged with another armful of gowns. Annabelle fidgeted, not wanting to encourage her mother to take steps that would further cement her decision to be married.

A conversation with one of her clients came to mind, a woman who had filed for divorce within weeks of marrying. She'd explained to Annabelle that she'd discovered her fiancé was cheating on her a few days before the wedding. When Annabelle had asked her why she hadn't simply canceled the ceremony, she'd shrugged and said, "My dress had a ten-foot train."

To fight the suffocation assailing her, Annabelle wandered away from the lace-bedecked mannequins in the direction of the lingerie racks, squirming. She'd purchased a couple of pairs of shorts, and could borrow tops from her mother's closet, but she still needed undies. And as luck would have it, the one bra spared the misdirection of the airline—the one she'd been wearing—had been the one with the wayward underwire. The darned thing had even set off the metal detector at the Detroit airport.

She fingered a simple, white cotton bra that would suffice, but recoiled when she turned over the price tag. *Ouch.* She'd gotten so used to squeaking by on a budget, she suspected that even if she graduated to a hefty paycheck someday, she'd always be a price-conscious shopper. Chewing on her lower lip, she moved to the clearance rack, which boasted less expensive but more *colorful* fare.

A backward glance convinced her Belle would be preoccupied for at least thirty minutes, so she launched a search mission for something remotely dignified. The first bra she selected was the correct size, but the red on black polka dots were a bit much, as was the next one, a filmy piece of yellow fabric shot with silver. A suitably boring beige number caught her eye, but the cups would have fit over her entire head. Her fingers stopped at a brown and black leopard print bra. Not bad—reasonably priced, dark, with good coverage, but a little… adventurous. Not that anyone would ever see it, unless they robbed the Sudsy Sam's Laundromat on Wednesday night during her delicate wash cycle.

Annabelle smirked. When the act of buying taboo underwear could lift a woman's spirits, her life was pretty dull. Then she shrugged. Dull was comfortable, and she wore it well.

On the other side of the rack, she found panties to match—a high-cut brief that looked as if it might pass the 'creep' test of sitting on an unpadded chair in a courtroom for taffy-long hours. She turned to a full-length tri-mirror and held up the garments over her overalls. Her hair had loosened from its clip, releasing long bangs she was trying to let grow out. Actually, the face-framing effect wasn't bad, which meant she would never be able to reproduce the look, not even with a dozen tools and two cans of hair spray. She worked her mouth from side to side, one plastic hanger under her chin and one mid-navel. The fabric was more sheer than she'd realized, but she liked the extra details—

A motion in the glass window to her left snagged her attention. She squinted, then walked closer. Martin Castleberry stood a few feet away on the other side of a glass divider, talking to—no, *hugging* a very young, very attractive woman. Incredulous, she pressed her nose against the glass. The neighboring store was a posh men's clothing boutique, and Martin's curvaceous companion seemed to be selecting ties for him, which apparently required that she touch him everywhere. Annabelle fumed—she'd caught him red-handed, the flirt!

Then in a flash her anger changed to triumph: *She'd caught him red-handed.* Now all she had to do was drag her mother over to witness his outrageous behavior, and this farce of a wedding would be off.

She turned on her heel and jogged back to the dress department where Belle seemed torn between a pale yellow suit and a coral-colored tea-length dress.

"Mother," she said in a sweet voice. "You'll never guess who's here."

"Who, dear?"

"Melvin."

Her mother's brow wrinkled.

"I mean Martin."

Belle brightened. "Really? How wonderful! Where is he?"

"Right next door at a men's clothing store—let's go say hello." Annabelle tucked the underwear beneath her arm and transferred a dress out of her mother's hand to the sales clerk's.

Her mother looked puzzled at her sudden burst of enthusiasm, but followed willingly enough when Annabelle grasped her elbow.

"Martin must be shopping for something new," Belle offered, giving a worried backward glance at the abandoned dresses.

"That's one way to put it," Annabelle muttered, urging her forward.

As they threaded through racks of evening gowns, dressy suits, and elaborate wraps, her heart beat faster with bittersweet anticipation. Her mother would be hurt at first, but would soon realize she was better off sans Martin Castleberry. What luck to have stumbled onto the man while he sported his true colors—at least Annabelle wouldn't wind up looking like the bad guy for saying less than favorable things about him. Cheered, she picked up her pace as she led her mother across the pale marble floor.

They exited the bridal shop and Annabelle practically dragged her mother into the men's clothing store. Thankfully, Martin and his young lady friend were still there. The woman was looping a green and navy striped tie around his neck and tying it with long, manicured fingers. She was smiling wide with her head tilted back, her long flaxen hair streaming nearly to her impossibly small waist. And Martin, ever the entertainer, seemed to be simply delighted with the ugly tie. Annabelle kept her gaze glued on his face for the sheer satisfaction of his expression when he noticed her mother.

A split second later he looked over the blonde's shoulder and his face erupted into a wide grin. "Belle! What a lovely surprise."

"Hello, my dear." Her mother smiled, seemingly unconcerned that another woman was draped over her intended. He sidestepped the young woman, and met Belle for a quick kiss on the mouth.

Martin extended a greeting to Annabelle, as if absolutely nothing was amiss. She could see why the man had been nominated for an Academy Award. "Martin," she said in her most innocent voice, "aren't you going to introduce your friend?"

As she expected, his brow furrowed in feigned perplexity. "My friend?" He followed Annabelle's pointed look toward the young woman who stood watching them with a questioning expression. "Oh, my *friend*." He beckoned the woman closer. A blip of panic assailed Annabelle when she saw the woman's salesclerk badge. "This is Suzanne Jacobson. Suzanne's father is my long-time friend and assistant—I was in the hospital waiting room when this young lady was born. Suzanne, may I present my fiancée, Belle Coakley, and her daughter, Annabelle."

The woman flashed a dazzling smile—Annabelle had never seen so many teeth in one mouth. "I'm pleased to meet you," Suzanne gushed. "I was helping Martin select a couple of ties while we waited for Clay." The woman pronounced the latter name with wistful familiarity.

Frustrated that her plan had been thwarted, and doubly irritated to meet one of what must be a long list of Clayton Castleberry admirers, Annabelle sent a withering glance toward a sock rack and muttered, "If I hear the name "Clay" one more time—"

"Careful," a male voice sounded near her ear, "my ears are already burning."

She wheeled, not entirely surprised to see Clay Castleberry, who seemed to pop up at the most inconvenient times. Dressed in classic dark jeans, a white ribbed T-shirt, and broken-in leather tennis shoes, Annabelle thought she had a good idea of what Martin might have looked like during his movie-making days. Clayton Castleberry was a striking man, an acknowledgment that only rankled her further.

The subject of her agitation swept his dark gaze over her overalls and quirked a brow. "They don't pay attorneys in Detroit enough to afford clothes?"

A flush scalded her neck. "The airline lost my luggage," she said through clenched teeth, feeling like a hobo next to the glittery, coiffed Suzanne, who paraded over to stand next to Annabelle, crowning the comparison.

"Hello, darlin'," the woman drawled to Clay, hiking out a rounded hip which had been vacuum-packed into a red skirt.

Clay's eyes followed her movement. "Hello, Suzanne. I haven't seen you in a while."

"That's your fault," she said silkily.

"I've been busy."

"Don't tell me you're getting married, too," she said, sounding wounded, then shot a suspicious glance toward Annabelle.

"No!" they said in unison.

Clay added a laugh, his voice casual. "I only came to help Dad select a tux."

"And I'm only here to help mother pick out a dress," Annabelle offered, hating that she felt the need to explain, and frowning at the older couple who stood engrossed in each other a few steps away. Belle straightened the hideous tie and Martin showered kisses upon her mother's hands. *Ugh.*

"Annabelle, dear," her mother said. "I'd like to show Martin that pink dress."

Martin flashed a charming smile. "You can stay with Clay, Annabelle, and give your opinion on the jacket style I picked out. Add the tie to my account, Suzanne. We'll be back in a few minutes."

They didn't even wait for an answer before strolling out of the shop, arm in arm. Annabelle gritted her teeth, lamenting the turn the day had taken. She'd been *so* close.

"Temper, temper," Clay chided.

She glared in his direction. "Shut. Up."

Suzanne glanced back and forth between them, then said, "I'll get the jacket Martin selected," and scampered away.

"You don't have to keep up the act around me," Clay said, folding his arms.

"What *are* you rambling about?" she asked, looking for somewhere to sit.

"I'm not convinced you're against this marriage as much as you pretend."

Her feet were killing her, and her head felt equally offended. She looked back to him and stepped closer, narrowing her eyes. "Mr. Castleberry, let me remind you that you dug a deep hole for yourself within the first ten minutes of our meeting." With every word, she inched toward him, her ire rising. "You are the most arrogant man I've ever had the displeasure of meeting. And I couldn't care less whether you find my behavior 'convincing,' because *you* have no say-so over any aspect of my life." She jabbed a finger in his chest, and winced when it met unyielding muscle. "Got it?"

"Excuse me," Suzanne said as she reappeared. Her voice had changed and she eyed Annabelle with unsettling smugness. A woman Annabelle recognized as the salesclerk who had assisted her mother stood behind the blonde.

"Yes?" Annabelle prompted, not bothering to hide her impatience.

"I'm afraid I'm going to have to ask you to come with me," Suzanne said. A grim-faced uniformed guard walked up and adopted a wide-legged stance.

"Is there a problem?" Annabelle asked.

"The problem," Suzanne said, punctuating every syllable with attitude, "is that you were seen shoplifting in the bridal store." She indicated the other salesclerk, who nodded curtly.

She knew her mouth had dropped open because she felt the cool air on her tongue. "*What?*"

"Let's have a look at what you're hiding under your arm," the guard said, obviously relishing the moment.

"Hiding?" Outrage billowed in her chest, stealing her voice. These uppity people were high-strung and paranoid. She threw her arms in the air with exaggeration, to prove them liars.

Then watched the brown and black sheer leopard-print bra and matching high-cut panties fall to the marble floor.

If the devil had appeared at that moment offering invisibility in exchange for her soul, Annabelle would have considered it. Pure mortification swept over her as her mind raced ahead, predicting how a shoplifting charge would affect her career. Didn't her employment contract negate the state's obligation to repay her loans if she were convicted of a crime? Without a good reference, she'd have a difficult time finding a decent job. Without a job, she'd never qualify to buy a house. Sheer panic forced defensive words out of her mouth. "Th-those things are n-not mine."

Suzanne scoffed, then bent and scooped the garments from the floor. Holding up the underwear, she scrutinized the orange clearance price tags with a look of disdain. "The bra appears to be your size."

High-necked blouses effectively hid her nerve rashes in court, but she suspected her yellow T-shirt offered little concealment today. "I m-mean, I browsed through the lingerie, and I p-picked up—I mean, I considered b-buying the underwear... then I saw Melvin, er, Martin from the other store, and I forgot... " She trailed off, gesturing with futility. "I... forgot I was holding them."

Her excuse sounded weak even to her own burning ears. Inexplicably, her eyes went to Clay's, hoping her expression wasn't as vulnerable as she felt. Of all the people she could make a fool out of herself in front of, he was the last person she'd have chosen. His gaze locked with hers. She'd expected smugness, but his narrowed dark eyes pierced her with—anger? He was embarrassed to be involved by association. Clay already thought the worst of her, so he'd probably be glad to see her carted off to jail.

Despite knowing the hostility he held for her and her mother, Clay was the closest thing she had to an ally at the moment, and Annabelle couldn't bring herself to look away. His gaze held her as surely as if a cable connected them. Strangely, she felt her body straining toward him, every hair, every nerve, every muscle, but she tensed to remain rooted. And stranger still, his eyes suddenly changed, softening in a way that caused her breath to catch in her chest.

For a few seconds, everything around them fell away, and voices retreated to a distant buzz. His jaw relaxed and she marveled that he looked younger and less intimidating. Still, something akin to fear crept into her heart—a sensation far more threatening than a trip to the hoosegow. Because she realized she was being given a glimpse of his compassion, an experience that left her feeling oddly privileged. Regardless of his feelings toward her, she somehow *knew* this man would not allow harm to come to her, and the knowledge warmed her.

He broke eye contact first, enabling her to breathe again, and put his hand on the guard's arm. "I believe we can clear up this matter to everyone's satisfaction. Ms. Coakley is an Atlanta native and a respected attorney in Detroit. She's visiting and is shopping with her mother, who is a close friend of my father, Martin Castleberry."

How had the rich texture of his voice had escaped her before now? He took the garments from Suzanne and held them at arm's length, the scanty garments incongruous next to his big hands. Annabelle swallowed. How could such a harmless act seem so intimate? Was she different? Was he? What had changed? Her cheeks burned from abject shame, both over her dilemma and her new awareness of Clayton Castleberry.

I-yie-yie. How quickly one's circumstances could deteriorate.

Clay stared at the silky underthings dangling from the tips of his fingers, a bit surprised that Annabelle's tastes in lingerie ran a little on the *savage* side. With little effort, he imagined the sheer bra and panties wrapped around her long-limbed body, her hair fanned out around her—

He gave himself a mental shake. When Suzanne accused Annabelle of shoplifting, his sense of vindication that she harbored an unsavory streak had been short-lived. One minute he'd been anticipating informing Martin that at least one of the Coakley women was a kleptomaniac, and the next minute Annabelle had turned her wide hazel eyes in his direction, stealing his momentum. Along with his ability to reason, apparently, because when the security guard emerged and passersby stopped to gawk, protective feelings had welled in his chest, prompting him to speak. He wanted to think the woman was smarter than to shoplift unmentionables, but could he still trust his instincts? And now the group stood staring at him, expecting…what?

He cleared his throat and continued, willing the right words to come. "And if Ms. Coakley says she forgot she was holding these items when she left the store, then that is exactly what happened." He met her gaze again and she squirmed, her face crimson. Suppressing a smile, he handed the items in question to the salesclerk from the bridal shop, then retrieved a black credit card from his wallet. "Put these things on my account, please."

"I'll pay for them—" Annabelle began, but stopped when he gave her a warning look and pressed her lips together. At least she knew when to hold her tongue…sometimes.

The older woman glanced at his credit card, then smiled with renewed respect. "Yes, Mr. Castleberry, right away."

The jab of annoyance at people's fickleness was superseded by the satisfaction that his name and his money afforded him the chance to bring Annabelle down from the high horse she'd ridden in on. Indeed, she was looking a bit subdued, her golden eyes soft and wary as she perused him, as if trying to determine his motives for rescuing her. He, meanwhile, wrestled with the same question.

Her expression riveted him, evoking visions of her lying beneath him, her eyes luminous with anticipation. But the imagined thrill of bedding Annabelle was soon displaced by the sobering reminder that many of life's greatest dangers came disguised in tempting packages. The woman was likely a petty thief who had designs on the Castleberry bank account, and had somehow managed to wangle a bit of sympathy from him. He only helped her in order to regain the upper hand, and to keep his father's name out of the mess.

Clay set his jaw against the irritating responses Annabelle Coakley evoked with a bat of her childishly long eyelashes. He had inherited his father's physical characteristics, but he did *not* possess the same blind weakness where pretty faces were concerned.

As if she'd read his mind, Annabelle mouthed 'thank you' even as she blinked rapidly. Clay frowned and studied her convincingly pale face, all the while massaging a sudden knot of anxiety above his topmost rib.

He was nothing like his father. Nothing at all.

"I can't believe it," Michaela said. "I just can't believe it."

"Mike, I wasn't *stealing* the underwear."

"Forget the stealing, I can't believe you were *buying* naughty underwear."

Annabelle sank back into the pillow on the couch and sighed. "It was a clearance sale."

"And Clayton Castleberry came to your rescue. Oh, how romantic!"

She fished a stale jellybean from a dish on the end table and popped it into her mouth. "There was nothing romantic about it. He was simply trying to keep his father's precious name out of a scandal. And he wanted to gloat."

"Still, you have to love the guy for taking care of everything."

Annabelle frowned, suddenly irritable. "I most certainly do not."

"Hey, quick—turn the channel to the EBC late talk show."

"Why?"

"I don't know what they're saying, but there's a picture of Martin Castleberry behind the comedian."

"Oh, great." She picked up the remote and selected the channel, leaning forward.

"Yeah," the comedian said over audience laughter. "Martin Casanova Castleberry is reported to be on his sixth, that's *sixth* trip down the aisle." The man hooted. "What is he, like a hundred and thirty years old? I can't get a date, and this man has a frequent fiancé card." The audience tittered as Annabelle's stomach rolled. "Oh, well that just proves the old adage that there's someone for everyone. Or, in Martin's case, *six* someones." More laughter sounded.

"Of course," the comedian continued, his hands in his pockets, "this wedding comes on the heels of Martin's recent settlement with a film company. What a coincidence, eh? I'm not saying the woman is a gold digger, but I heard she carries a pickaxe and rides a mule." He shook his head as he moved on to another topic.

"Don't let it get to you," Michaela said. "It must have been a slow news day. He wasn't even funny, the jerk. And it's an obscure show—no one saw it, probably."

"*We* saw it."

"Poor Belle."

"Mom will be a laughingstock if she marries that man. It's just a matter of time before pictures of her are plastered on television," Annabelle muttered, turning down the volume.

"How are plans for the big wedding coming along?"

She groaned. "Well, I helped her whittle down the guest list to a mere one hundred."

"Wow."

"They're supposed to be married by Martin's pool on Saturday."

"That's four days from now."

"Don't remind me. She's ordering the cake and food tomorrow, and Martin's publicist arranged for a photographer." She popped another jellybean into her mouth. "The beast is gaining momentum."

"What about the dresses?"

"She picked out the dresses today while I was being threatened with handcuffs."

"How fun! What color?"

Annabelle rolled her eyes—Mike was such a girly-girl. "Pink."

Predictably, Michaela squealed. "Oh, they sound fantastic."

Inexplicably, the image of the beautifully simple white gown in the glass case rose in her mind. Then she shook herself. "Mike, I think you're forgetting the objective here is to *stop* the wedding."

"But it's such good practice."

"For what—having a nervous breakdown?"

Her friend laughed. "For your own wedding, silly."

She raised her eyebrows. "Do you know something I don't?"

"No, but if a whirlwind romance can happen to your mother, it can happen to you."

Annabelle scoffed. "Mike, if I were going to get married—which I'm not—I would hope I'd have enough sense—which I do—not to exchange vows with a man I barely know."

"But haven't you ever met someone and instantly felt as if you knew them?"

She hedged and hunted for a green jellybean. "That only happens in the movies. Black and white movies, I might add. And besides, just because you feel like you know someone doesn't guarantee you'll like them."

Mike sighed. "Maybe, but a girl can hope."

"Well, this girl has to figure out a plan before tomorrow. Buying dresses is bad enough, but I'm not about to let her put down a deposit with a caterer."

"Isn't Martin paying for everything?"

"She wouldn't let him buy the dress, and I insisted on paying for mine." She shifted, humming with disapproval. "His son owns the house he's living in—I'm starting to think this Castleberry character might be marrying my mother for *her* money."

"I thought he just got some sort of big lawsuit settlement."

"Maybe, but who knows how many bills the man had, or how many bad habits he has to support?"

"But you said he bought her a rock of an engagement ring."

She thought of the modestly beautiful ring her mother had given her wrapped in her dresser drawer, and her heart squeezed. "It's an unsightly boulder, and he probably bought it on credit." Annabelle snapped her fingers. "Or it's fake!"

"How can you tell?"

"Outside of taking it to a jeweler, I don't know."

"Do you think Belle would mind if it's phony?"

"Probably not if he told her up front."

"But if it's fake and he *didn't* tell her—"

"Then she'd know she couldn't trust him!" Annabelle said, whooping. "Mike, you're a genius." She tossed down another jellybean.

"Can I have a raise?"

"Sure, as soon as *I* get one."

"Call me tomorrow with an update. And tell Mr. Clayton Castleberry the next time he's in Detroit, there's a nice, available, *lonely* woman in our building who's in dire need of a hero."

She fought an exasperated smile. "Mike, for the last time, I'm not interested in the guy."

"I was talking about *me*, boss."

"Oh…right."

CHAPTER SEVEN

CLAY RUBBED HIS EYES against the morning light streaming through the curtains. He didn't mind losing sleep—he thrived on five hours a night—but he *did* mind losing sleep over a slip of a freckle-faced girl. Annabelle Coakley frustrated him beyond belief with her argumentative, independent ways. She'd already caused him more headaches and energy than was warranted.

In fact, after watching a dolt of a comedian last night use Martin as a weak punch line, and while contemplating the ceiling fixture in the wee hours of the morning, he'd decided he'd wasted enough time in Atlanta. Maybe he'd jumped to conclusions concerning the Coakley women...maybe he would simply let Martin take his chances...maybe the three of them deserved each other.

The early morning light glinted off his platinum watch and he smiled. He might be able to catch a plane back to Paris this afternoon. Paris, where the women dressed like women—instead of wearing scruffy overalls—and did not live to aggravate the men around them. And since his father would be preoccupied with his new marriage, he might look into extending the lease on the Paris flat for himself.

Enormously cheered, Clay swung his legs over the edge of the bed and stretched away the remnants of what little sleep he'd snatched. He would tie up a loose end or two, and be eating fresh croissants by tomorrow morning. He retrieved his phone and punched in Henry's number. The private investigator lived on an intravenous drip of black coffee, and appeared to be nocturnal. Sure enough, he answered on the first ring.

"Henry, this is Clay Castleberry. Give me what you have on the Coakley women."

"Mornin' to you, too," Henry said, rustling papers in the background.

Clay moved to the open window, parted the curtains and looked out over the Coakley house. Which room was hers? Was she still slumbering in a tousled bed?

Henry coughed, then cleared his throat noisily. "Not much on the older lady. Fifty-six years old, married to a small-time attorney for thirty-odd years, never employed outside the home, no relationships since her husband died that I could dig up. Goes to church, volunteers at the library, with no evident vices unless you count Bingo at the garden club." He laughed, then slurped something, probably java.

Clay strained for some sign of life at the windows, baffled when he realized his heart raced at the thought of a taboo glimpse of her. Disgusted with himself, he started to turn, but a movement at a window of the smaller house stopped him. The curtains parted and Annabelle appeared, her arms pushing aside the window coverings to allow the sun into her room. Crazily, his chest tightened.

"What about the younger one?" he asked Henry. Why was it almost painful to even say her name?

"Annabelle?"

"Right." He wasn't sure from this distance, but he thought he saw the flash of white teeth. She was smiling—would wonders never cease?

"Not much back on her yet, but I was able to tail her and her mother most of yesterday. Lunch at Lenox Mall, during which she showed her mother an article from *America's News*. They had a disagreement—the young gal raised her voice and said she was worried about something. I looked up the article; it was a piece that ran a few months back about the settlement your father received from the lawsuit. Want a copy?"

Stunned, Clay could only grunt. Next door Annabelle lifted the window and leaned out, resting on her elbows. She must have been worried that her mother might not get a chunk of the settlement money. His initial suspicions about her had been right after all...so why did he feel betrayed?

"After breakfast, the women did lots of shopping, more looking than buying. Even tried on fur coats—in the summer, can you believe it?"

She wore yellow pajamas. Her arms gleamed bare and her hair piled around her shoulders in a sleep-mussed stack. "Go on," Clay managed past his thickened tongue.

"Then they met up with you and your father—nice of you to bail her out of that shoplifting mess, by the way."

Not nice—stupid. How *stupid* of him to bail her out of that shoplifting mess. "You were there?"

"Yeah, trying on cuff links."

Impressive. Of course, he'd been so distracted by Little Miss Innocent, he wouldn't have noticed if the President himself had walked in to buy a tie. "What about after they left us?"

"They went to two car lots and test drove luxury sedans. Sounds to me like they're planning to come into some money soon."

Clay's throat constricted as she stretched her arms high and tilted her face upward. No wonder she was so happy—she and her mother were on the verge of gaining access to a small fortune. To avoid detection, he dropped the curtain, then managed to thank Henry and asked him to report back when he received more information on the younger Ms. Coakley. After disconnecting the call, he wiped a fine sheen of perspiration from his brow and peeked through the slit in the curtains.

The window remained open, but Annabelle had disappeared. Sheer white panels floated out over the sill, riding on a summer breeze. Clay swallowed the bitter taste in the back of his throat, trying to block out the image of her golden eyes mocking him. Over the last several hours, he'd even imagined that he might be falling—

No. Not falling. Stumbling, maybe, because he thought he'd seen something in her eyes that had spoken to him.

Perhaps he'd inherited more of his father's weaknesses than he cared to admit.

Clay cursed and closed the window with a bang.

"Annabelle, what happened yesterday between you and Clay?"

Annabelle hurriedly dropped the filmy leopard-print undergarments back into the drawer, then turned and leaned against the dresser.

Her mother stood in the doorway of Annabelle's old bedroom, wrapped in a satiny robe, holding two cups of morning tea.

Annabelle donned a wide-eyed expression. "Happened?" Her voice emerged a tad on the squeaky side.

"Yes, dear. Between you and Clay."

"Yesterday?"

Belle nodded, her face a mask of patience as she handed over one of the steaming mugs.

Annabelle stalled by blowing onto the surface of the milky liquid, then taking a sip. She'd lain awake some of the night pondering Clay's motivation for rescuing her from the embarrassing predicament at the shopping mall. But she'd lain awake *most* of the night pondering her dawning attraction to the confounding man. Darn Mike for stirring up these ridiculous fantasies with all her silly talk.

"Annabelle?"

Glancing up guiltily, she knew her mother had already zeroed in on the circles beneath her eyes, but were her sudden disconcerting feelings toward Clay equally as obvious? "I'm not sure what you mean, Mom."

"I mean it was obvious that the two of you had words, and frankly, I'm disappointed that you're not making more of an effort to get along with Clay."

She gulped her tea, scalding her tongue. She and Clay had exchanged scarcely two words while he was being fitted for the tuxedo jacket. She'd found a corner from which to observe him and the eager Suzanne, and tried to ignore the flashes of unease every time the blonde's hands lingered at his neck, his lapel, his waist. Annabelle did make one amazing discovery: When Clay smiled, the unfamiliar expression had a bizarre effect on her pulse. And he seemed to smile easily with his longtime acquaintance. Apparently, he reserved his disdain for herself and her mother.

And rather than diminishing, her embarrassment over the shoplifting event grew exponentially as she replayed each agonizing moment over and over—he'd seen her *underwear*, for heaven's sake. Although she'd braced herself for Clay's smug retelling of the incident when their parents rejoined them, he hadn't mentioned it. He'd politely complimented Belle on the pink dresses she'd chosen, reminded his father they had an appointment in Midtown, then left without making eye contact.

Walking over to the window she'd opened, Annabelle shrugged lightly at her mother's observation. "In case you hadn't noticed, Clay isn't as friendly as his father. I can't make the man like me."

"But you could be more gracious to both of the men who will soon be part of our family," Belle chided.

She looked above the tree line to the coral-colored house, feeling strangely drawn to the young man living there temporarily. Had he given her a passing thought since yesterday? Deciding to change the troubling subject, Annabelle turned with a smile. "Mom, I never asked you how Melvin proposed."

"It's Martin, dear." Belle sat on the edge of the bed and dimpled. "He took me to my favorite Italian restaurant—they serve the most incredible vanilla mints wrapped in silver foil with their coffee." A faraway look came into her eyes and she sighed. "We had a wonderfully romantic meal, and when the waiter brought our mints, my engagement ring was around one of them."

"That *is* romantic," Annabelle mumbled begrudgingly, wondering from which movie he'd stolen that scene. "The stone in your ring is huge," she said, taking a seat next to Belle and lifting her mother's hand for a better look. Under the soft overhead light, the oval stone reflected a spectrum of colors. Injecting a teasing tone into her voice, she asked, "Are you sure it's real?"

Belle's laughter trilled through the room. "Of course it's real, dear."

"Did he buy it from a jeweler nearby?"

Her mother looked puzzled. "I didn't ask. Why?"

"Well, I... " She glanced around the room and her eyes fell upon her dresser, sparking an idea. "I thought we could take Daddy's engagement ring to a jeweler and have it resized."

Belle smiled in agreement. "That's a lovely idea, and there's a jeweler who repaired a gold chain of mine just a couple of miles from the caterer."

"Good, because it looks like a prong has moved on the ring Martin gave you."

She pointed and Belle squinted.

"Really? I can't see up close without my glasses. Oh, my, I'd hate to lose the stone."

"I'll drop you off at the caterer's and take the rings to the jeweler, then we can go back to the car lot and take a second look at that green sedan."

Belle gave a dismissive wave. "Dear, I simply won't permit you to buy me a new car."

"Mother, the car is hardly new, and you can't keep driving Dad's old tank with the engine light coming on all the time. Why didn't you tell me?"

"Because I knew you'd make a fuss. Besides, you need your money for your new house...don't you?"

Annabelle detected a note of curiosity in Belle's voice, which she ignored. Her mother might worry more if she knew where the money had come from. She patted her mother's knee with affection. "I insist on buying you a decent car, and I'll still have enough left for my down payment." Her heart swelled with pride—her father would definitely approve. Martin Castleberry be damned—she could take care of her mother.

"Speaking of your new house, you'll be needing some furniture."

Belle's voice and expression were so innocent, Annabelle was instantly alert. "Well, the bedroom suite I bought for my apartment is still in great condition, but I thought I'd have my couch reupholstered."

"I'm giving you mine."

"Your couch?"

"My furniture."

She stared for a few seconds, then laughed. "Mom, that's ridiculous. You can't give me your furniture—what on earth will you use?" As soon as the words left her mouth, she realized what her mother was leading up to.

"I'm selling the house, dear."

Her heart jumped to her throat. "What?"

"Martin and I don't need two homes, so it only makes sense to sell this one."

After a shaky inhale, Annabelle touched her mother's arm. "Mom, you can't sell this house. Besides, Martin doesn't own the house he lives in—Clay does. You don't want to be at *that* man's mercy, do you?"

"Martin is buying it back from him."

She pursed her mouth, realization dawning. "With the proceeds from *this* house?"

"It's only fair that I contribute some," Belle insisted, "since Martin wants my name to also be on the title."

"How generous of him to offer," she said dryly. "Mom, he's taking advantage of you!"

"Nonsense."

Panic rolled in Annabelle's stomach and she stood. "I think you and I should go back to Detroit—immediately."

"What?" Belle laughed, standing. "I'm getting married Saturday!"

"Mom, we need to talk."

Belle wagged her index finger. "I know this has been a shock, dear, and I'm sorry, but you're not changing my mind. Now let's get dressed—the real estate agent will be here in a few minutes." Her mother sashayed out of the room, her high-heeled house shoes clacking against the wooden floor.

Annabelle's mind spun as she watched her mother walk away. She wanted to cry out, but her voice had fled and her limbs were numb. She'd never felt more helpless in her life, because she was certain that Martin Castleberry was marrying her mother for what bit of money her parents had managed to save over their lifetime. What was she going to do? From the hall she heard the spray of her mother's shower, and the dull click of the glass door closing. She gulped her tea, wincing when the liquid washed over her burned tongue. Was there such a thing as tough love for parents?

The doorbell rang and her pulse shot up. Not only had the agent arrived early, but since her mother was indisposed, she was going to have to play hostess. But as she pulled on a robe, an idea occurred to her and she brightened. *Her mother was indisposed.* She trotted to the door, painting on a smile for the suited woman who stood on the doorstep. "Hello. You must be from the Realty company."

"Yes, I'm Brenda Morra. Are you Mrs. Coakley?"

"I'm her daughter. Mother is busy at the moment."

The woman stretched her neck to peek around Annabelle. "This is such a lovely home."

"Thanks. Could you come back next week?"

Her smile dropped. "I was under the impression Mrs. Coakley was leaving town on her honeymoon soon and wouldn't be back for a few weeks."

"Not if I can help it," Annabelle muttered.

"Excuse me?"

"It looks as if her plans might change," she said, with the most convincing smile she could muster. Behind her, the sound of her mother's shower kicked off. "One of us will be in touch soon," Annabelle added, stepping back. "Thank you for stopping by."

"But—"

"We'll call you," she assured the woman, waving as she closed the door. Then she leaned against the door and blew her too-long bangs in the air.

"Annabelle, dear, was that someone at the door?" her mother yelled from the bathroom.

"The real estate agent," she replied, choosing her words carefully as she moved down the hall. "She, um, rescheduled."

Belle stuck her head out of the bathroom, her pale hair dripping, her face a mask of concern. "For when?"

"I didn't know your schedule, so I told her we'd be in touch."

"You should have asked me while she was here, dear."

Annabelle crossed her fingers behind her back. "She was in a hurry."

Belle disappeared back into the bathroom. "Remind me to call her when we return from running our errands."

She looked heavenward and mouthed, *That was close.*

"Oh," her mother's voice echoed in the bathroom, "I forgot to mention that Martin and Clay are taking us to dinner this evening."

"Dinner?" Her heart tripped faster. "Why?"

Belle's laughter vibrated. "Because we have to eat, dear, and we could do worse than eating in the company of two attractive men."

She groaned and sagged against the wall in the hallway, exhausted before their day had even begun. Right now, her seventy-hours-a-week job seemed like nirvana.

"Annabelle." Her mother's head appeared again. "It would mean so much to me if you would try to be friends with Clay." She ducked back into the bathroom, and her voice floated out, muffled. "But believe me, after spending time with the man, I understand your reluctance. He has such a difficult personality."

Annabelle worked her mouth from side to side and studied her rumpled reflection in the mirror over the hall table. "Well, after all, he did leave a business deal in Paris to come back and attend the wedding."

"I suppose. But *arrogant*, mercy, mercy."

Her hair definitely needed a trim. "I know, but at least he has accomplishments to back up his attitude."

"And he seems kind of brooding to me."

Annabelle shrugged. "It worked in *Wuthering Heights*."

"And now that I think about it, he's not nearly as handsome as Martin was at that age."

Annabelle pursed her lips and leaned close to the mirror. How long since she'd last plucked her eyebrows? "He's really not *bad* looking when he smiles."

"Ha! And when is that?"

She stuck her tongue in her cheek, remembering their heated exchanges with a little smirk. "He has a subtle sense of humor. You have to get to know him, I guess." Then she straightened. "Not that I do. Know him, that is."

"Well, thanks for the insight, dear. Tonight we'll both try to be more open-minded, hm?"

The blow dryer whirred to life, and Annabelle headed toward her room, dragging her feet. After stubbing her toe, she hopped into her bedroom and landed on her bed, more irritated than ever. Her skin felt bothersome, as if she might be coming down with something—which would explain the general feeling of detachment from her body. She just wanted to close her eyes and have everything the way it was before her mother called last Friday to break the news of the wedding.

And if she didn't have enough to worry about, now she was going to have to spend this evening staring across the table at Clay. Annabelle rolled to her back and groaned.

What on earth was she going to wear?

CHAPTER EIGHT

"WE CAN HAVE THE RING SIZED while you wait, ma'am," the man said with a courteous nod.

Knowing her mother would probably be meeting with the caterer for at least another hour, Annabelle nodded. "Fine."

The man signaled a young woman and handed the ring off to her with instructions, then turned back to Annabelle with a huge smile. "Now then, perhaps I can show you some of our new pieces while you're waiting?"

Nervous about simply whipping out her mother's ring and asking if the stone was real, Annabelle nodded and allowed the man to show her an array of tennis bracelets. She even humored him by trying on a few, although the only piece she found remotely interesting was a simple silver bangle with a raised griffin design. After a few minutes, she scanned the shop for eavesdroppers, relieved to find only one other customer, a man trying on watches on the opposite side of the showroom.

Annabelle thanked the man for showing her the bracelets, then cleared her throat. "Sir, I, um, was wondering if you might tell me how much a piece of jewelry is worth."

He nodded. "Certainly we offer appraisals, although it would take at least forty-eight hours to process a piece for purposes of insuring."

A flush warmed her neck as she fidgeted. Finally, she withdrew the ring box from her purse. "The truth is, I only need for you to tell me if the stone in this ring is as valuable as, um…"

"As you've been led to believe?" he inquired with a twinkle in his eye.

She coughed lightly into her hand, then nodded.

He pulled a jeweler's monocle from his pocket. "Then let's have a quick look."

Annabelle chewed on her bottom lip as the man scrutinized the ring and hummed noncommittally. After a full minute, he lowered the eyeglass, his expression unreadable. "A gift?"

She nodded again.

The man gave her a tight smile and returned the ring. "Miss, not only is the stone genuine, but based upon my hurried observation, it's of uncommonly good quality."

She couldn't keep her mouth from turning down at the corners, and the man seemed surprised. "Not the news you were hoping for, ma'am?"

"No," she murmured, then added hastily, "I mean yes." She managed a happy expression. "Of course." Darn it—the sole reason she'd been looking forward to dinner tonight with the Castleberrys was to triumphantly expose the ring as a fake and begin to unravel the fabric of lies that the senior Castleberry had managed to wrap around her mother's eyes.

"Ah, and here's your other ring, ma'am, freshly sized and cleaned." He handed Annabelle the engagement ring her father had given her mother. A lump formed in her throat as she pushed the ring over her knuckle. *Anna, promise me you'll look after your mother if something happens to me.*

"I'm trying, Dad," she whispered, then thanked the man and paid for the re-sizing. With heavy feet, she walked in the direction of the exit, distracted by the unfamiliar weight of the ring on her left hand, saddened now that she'd had it cut down to fit her finger when it truly belonged on her mother's. Now what? Her mother was marrying Melvin Castleberry in mere days, and it seemed as if there was little she could do about it. Oh, well, if the caterer ran true to form, maybe he'd already aggravated Belle enough to reconsider the entire production. Regardless, she needed to get back to her mother as soon as possible to ensure she didn't go overboard.

Weddings—bah!

The driving summer shower that had blown in only added insult to injury. Without an umbrella, she held her purse over her head and jogged to her mother's blue Buick. After dropping the keys twice, she fumbled her way into the car. Her hair dripping wet, she sat behind the gigantic steering wheel and shivered for a few seconds, then turned over the engine. The best thing about Belle's car was that it was so huge, other drivers got out of the way—a phenomenon in Atlanta.

But she'd traveled no farther than the other side of the shopping center when the engine light flashed on, and the car died. She turned the key and the engine whined, but wouldn't turn over, not even on the second or the third try. Annabelle thumped the steering wheel, then gave in to the ridiculous tears she'd been fighting for what seemed like days. Belle's dogged determination to marry had her on edge, and the sleepless nights she'd spent dissecting her puzzling encounters with Clay hadn't helped matters. And now this.

She lay her head down on the steering wheel and bawled.

Clay was on his way back from checking the painting progress on his condo when his phone rang. He picked it up and saw Henry's name on the caller ID screen. Tensing for more bad news, he pushed a button. "Yeah, Henry, what's up?"

"It's the girl," the private investigator said. "She's having car trouble and it's raining like hell. Call me old-fashioned, but I feel like I should help her or something."

Remembering the look of her big hazel eyes when she thought she might be arrested in the department store, Clay could sympathize with Henry's instincts, but he didn't want the man to blow his cover. "Where is she?"

"Sherell Shopping Center on Buice Road."

Clay looked around to get his bearings. "I'm not far from there—in fact, I'm driving into rain now. I'll say I just happened by."

"She's in a blue Buick in front of the jeweler's."

"Jeweler's?"

"Yeah, she had an engagement ring sized for herself—"

Clay scowled. Was Annabelle engaged to that Mike fellow he overheard her mother talking about? "Are you certain?"

"Yeah, I heard everything. And she had the ring your dad gave to her mother—she wanted the jeweler to tell her how much it was worth."

Clay's heart fell to his stomach—he'd seen the bill for the ring, and the bauble was worth a hefty sum. "Really."

"I didn't catch what she said, but she looked disappointed with whatever the fellow told her."

Clay's heart fell to his knees. A hefty sum, but not as much as she'd anticipated, obviously. "Thanks, Henry. By the way, Dad and I are having dinner with them this evening, so skip the surveillance and try to get me some details of the daughter's personal life in Michigan—relationships with men, that kind of thing." He needed the information to help protect his father.

Not to satisfy his own curiosity.

"Sure thing, Clay."

He disconnected the call, chewing on the inside of his cheek. Annabelle couldn't have taken the ring without her mother's knowledge, so Belle was in on it, too. Were they planning to hock the ring? Or were they simply using it as a barometer to estimate his father's wealth? He remembered her frightened expression in the department store and scoffed. A mother and daughter team, playing up to father and son. No wonder he was starting to feel soft toward Annabelle—she'd probably planned it that way, the schemer. The more he thought about the way she'd wormed her way into his subconscious, the more irritated he became, taking solace only in the fact that *if* he had yielded to her wiles, it was because she was such a pro.

Within a couple of minutes, he had the shopping center in sight, and the stalled car wasn't hard to find considering the line of traffic detouring around the sides. Impatient drivers delivered punctuated honks at the woman sitting inside behind the wheel, apparently waiting out the worst of the summer storm. Despite his hardened resolve, Clay experienced a pang of compassion, thinking he certainly wouldn't want his sister—if he had one—to be in the same predicament.

While he waited to turn in, she suddenly sprang from the car and ran through the rain in the direction of a nearby bank, ducking beneath the drive-through canopy to shake herself like a dark, wet collie. He hated the protective feelings that welled in his chest at the bedraggled sight of her. Clay pulled into the drive-through corridor, then buzzed down his window, forcing surprise into his voice. "Annabelle?"

Annabelle winced when she recognized Clay's voice, then slowly turned. It was him, all right, tucked inside his splendid luxury sedan, gorgeous, grinning... and dry.

"Hello," she said with as much nonchalance as she could muster while shoving long wet bangs out of her eyes. Her cotton shorts and thin T-shirt clung to her.

"Having car trouble?"

"Yes."

He looked at her for a few seconds, then beckoned her with a jerk of his head. "Well, get in."

Torn between exasperation and gratitude, she ran around the front of his car and slid into the passenger seat. The door closed with a vacuum seal. Her wet skin squeaked against the gray leather seat, and her chest rose and fell quickly as she recovered from the brief exertion. She felt like a drowned cat. Clay, on the other hand, was unruffled and impossibly handsome in jeans and a navy polo shirt. Seeing him again both soothed and rankled her in a way she couldn't explain, so she reasoned she wasn't glad to see him, but simply glad she wouldn't have to wait on a wrecker for a ride.

"Thanks," she murmured, smoothing a hand over her hair. "Out running errands?"

"I, um, had to make a deposit," he said, gesturing to the bank.

"Nineteen thousand nine hundred dollars?" she asked sweetly.

Clay frowned. "You're soaked."

Realizing her dripping self wasn't exactly good for the interior, she said, "Sorry about your upholstery."

He shook his head to dismiss her worry, then leaned toward her. For a split second, Annabelle's breath caught in her throat—he was going to kiss her again. Her mouth twitched in anticipation.

"I usually keep a golf towel in here," he said, unlatching the glove compartment. "Ah." He withdrew a small white cloth and offered it to her.

Her embarrassment slowed her reflexes.

He shook the towel. "It's clean."

She accepted it with a tight smile and sopped up the wetness on her arms.

"What happened to your mother's car?"

"The engine light has been coming on lately. This time it came on and the engine died."

"That doesn't sound safe."

"No, but Mom's getting a new car soon." She was taking Belle to the car lot tomorrow to get that used sedan, whether she liked it or not.

He pulled out into the rain and maneuvered his car nose to nose with the Buick. "In case your battery just needs to be jumped," he answered her puzzled look.

"I don't think it's the battery," she said. "The engine won't turn over."

"Could you be out of gas?" His tone held a note of amused chauvinism that needled her.

"No, I'm not out of gas," she assured him in an appropriately sing-songy feminine voice.

"I'll take a quick look under the hood unless you'd rather I take you home first."

She lifted one eyebrow. "Wow, a venture capitalist *and* a mechanic."

He belted out a hearty laugh that surprised her, throaty and lingering. A rush of pleasure pulsed through her to be able to evoke that laugh from such a guarded man. Immediately, she wanted to hear it again.

Clay held out his hand, giving her a good look at a perplexing row of calluses. He hadn't gotten them from carrying around his briefcase. "Your keys?"

She dug in her canvas purse, finally fishing the keys from the farthest corner. "Actually, Mother is waiting for me at the caterer's. I was going back to pick her up as soon as I, um, ran a couple of errands." She gave in to a clammy shiver, embarrassed anew at the picture she must present—the man probably thought she was the most accident-prone person walking.

"Here," he said, reaching into the back seat where a stack of clothes lay in plastic dry cleaner's bags. He removed a black cotton sweater from a hanger and handed it to her. "A little big for you, but it'll keep you warm."

"Th-thank you," she stammered. The sweater was soft and welcoming, but she bit her lower lip, hesitant to put on an article of the man's clothing, especially after she glanced at the label. *I-yie-yie.*

He turned a knob that warmed the blast of air coming from the vents. "Stay put and I'll see what I can do."

When the door closed behind him, she draped the sweater around her shoulders as she watched him in the side mirror. If possible, the rain was coming down even harder. He circled around to the back of his car and withdrew a ball cap from the trunk, which he jammed on his head. Then he strode to the driver's side of her mother's car where he unlocked the door, and lowered himself inside. A minute later, he exited and raised the hood of the Buick. His back muscles moved under the damp shirt, making her very aware of the contained power of his body.

Protected…she felt protected.

Shaken by the realization that such a simple act of assistance could affect her, Annabelle busied her hands drying herself with the towel he'd given her. She even managed to squeeze some moisture from the ends of her hair, then unfolded the towel and stared at the pale green logo. *Kenton Keys Country Club, Atlanta.* She shook her head at the reminder of a lifestyle to which he was so accustomed, wondering how much he spent on greens fees in a year's time. Different worlds, she reminded herself. A relationship between them would never wor—

The driver's door opened, startling her, and Clay swung inside, shrugging off moisture, then tossed his cap onto the back floorboard. His face looked grim, and water dripped from the end of his nose. "The engine won't turn over."

Annabelle laughed and passed him the towel. "Told you so."

"Might be the alternator," he said, wiping his neck. He held up his phone. "I can call a repair shop I've used."

"If they work on Mercedes, they might not take Mom's car."

He shook his head as he put his car into gear. "It's not a dealership—they fixed a fuel line on my pickup."

She blinked. "Pickup? You own a pickup truck?"

"You sound surprised."

"No," she said quickly. "Well, yes. You just don't strike me as someone who would need a pickup."

He gave her a pointed look. "Maybe you don't know me as well as you think." He punched in a phone number, then proceeded to arrange for the car to be towed and repaired as soon as was humanly possible.

His words vibrated in her head as she watched him talk and move, noting the way his wet dark hair curled over his forehead and around his ears. *Maybe I don't know you…and maybe I'd like to.* The revelation stunned her, and her defenses immediately sprang up. The most stupid, destructive thing she could do to herself would be to fall for Clay Castleberry.

"Someone will be here in a couple of minutes," he said, putting away his phone. "Then we'll pick up your mother, unless you need to run more errands."

Annabelle's gaze involuntarily flew to her mother's ring twinkling on her left hand. "No, I was finished."

"Hey," Clay said mildly, following her glance. "That's new."

"Um, not really." She was hesitant to tell him she'd accepted her mother's old ring since he might see it as a sign of relenting to the idea of a union between their families.

"Oh?" he asked, then reached forward to grasp the knuckle of her ring finger. His touch sent a bolt of awareness through her hand as he eyed the modest but brilliant stone. "I hadn't noticed you wearing it before."

"I, um, had to have it resized."

"Ah. I'm just surprised—I assumed your occupation had turned you against marriage."

Annabelle almost frowned in confusion, then realized with a start that he thought *she* was engaged. Laughter bubbled in her throat—although the idea was absurd, what perfect insulation to cool the increasing heat between them. Because even if Clay entertained the slightest intention of kissing her again, he certainly wouldn't waste his time on a taken woman. "Well," she said breezily, tucking a strand of wet hair behind a wet ear, "maybe you don't know me as well as you think."

"Touché." The corners of his mouth turned down. "I assume you were informed about our plans this evening."

So he wasn't looking forward to having dinner, she realized with the most irksome little tickle of disappointment. Annabelle managed a casual shrug. "Since our parents insist on dragging us along, perhaps we can try to reason with them and put a stop to this ridiculous wedding."

"Right," he replied as a wrecker pulled up next to them. "Let's try to make the best of an unpleasant situation."

Annabelle manufactured a shaky smile. "Yes, let's."

CHAPTER NINE

"PROMISE ME, CLAY," his father said as they stood at the restaurant bar, "that you'll be on your best behavior tonight."

Clay scowled. "In case you hadn't noticed, Dad, I'm no longer a child to be reprimanded." Not that his father had reprimanded him as a child, either—Martin hadn't been around enough to dole out discipline.

Martin sighed. "Son, if you're angry with me over this marriage, fine, but don't take it out on Belle, and more specifically, Annabelle."

"Annabelle?"

His father arched an eyebrow. "Belle and I would like for the two of you to try to get along."

"Gee, I thought it was just this afternoon that I gave her a ride when her car broke down."

"And you've been in a foul mood ever since."

Clay banged his drink glass down on the bar. "I can't help it—there's something about that woman I don't like."

Martin looked past his shoulder, then stood abruptly. "I can't imagine what on earth it would be."

Alerted by the tone in his father's voice, Clayton turned, and all the moisture left his mouth. Annabelle and her mother stood in the entrance to the restaurant bar, and while Belle was certainly attractive for her age, every male head in the room had turned to admire Annabelle.

She wore a yellow sleeveless dress that hit her lean leg well above the knee, and high-heeled silver sandals with an ankle strap. He had never fancied himself as having a shoe fetish, but he was riveted to those ankle straps—although admittedly the slim ankles they enclosed might have provided the allure. And her hair...her hair was pulled back smoothly from her face and formed a loose knot at the nape of her neck. Unframed, her face was radiant, notwithstanding the little frown that furrowed her brow as she swept her gaze over the room. His pulse quickened absurdly at the fleeting realization that she was looking for him.

A square of colored paper he recognized as the valet ticket floated unnoticed from her hand to the floor and at least a half-dozen men moved toward her, spurring him into action. He covered the area in four easy strides and snatched the ticket from the hand of a hopeful looking fellow. "Thank you."

As he turned to Annabelle, he was shaken by the urge to stake his territory in the room full of men who were on the prowl. "Hello."

"Hi," she said with the briefest of smiles. Her eyes glittered golden beneath the subdued lighting. She looked like a movie star.

He held up the valet ticket. "I'll hang on to this for you."

She nodded and he detected a wonderful clean scent floating around her—like floral soap and fruity shampoo. A woman's grooming had always been the most intriguing mystery to him—the hours spent in the bathroom among fragrant potions to emerge soft-skinned and pink-cheeked and sweet-smelling. It was one of his fondest memories of his mother. Whether wearing an evening gown or an old gardening shirt, she always smelled like a lady. Annabelle's skin gleamed with dewy moisture, evoking images of her shoulder-deep in a bubble bath, a vision that stirred him.

His father's voice sounded behind him, and he forced himself to focus on the words. "... just called our name, son. Our table is ready."

The spell broken, he turned to see Martin and Belle walking ahead of them. He swept his arm in front of Annabelle. "After you." Then he fell in step a half-pace behind her, his hand skimming her lower back, just in case she lost her way following the hostess and their parents. "I see the airline found your luggage."

Annabelle crinkled her nose. "Not yet. Counting that pink bridesmaid getup, this makes two useless dresses I've had to buy and will probably never wear again."

"You don't dress up for your fiancé?" he asked casually.

"W-well..."

"Then I'm flattered."

She sniffed daintily, her gaze straight ahead. "Don't be."

On the other hand, he conceded wryly, good old Mike would be privy to that sheer little bra and panty ensemble. He glanced at her left hand, surprised to find it naked. "Speaking of which, where's your ring?"

Her step faltered as she covered her left hand with her right. "I must have forgotten it."

Clay pursed his lips, thinking Annabelle probably slid the ring on and off at whim. He wondered if Mike in Michigan knew what kind of fickle female he was engaged to. Then he frowned. Perhaps Annabelle's betrothed was some poor unassuming older man who, like his father, didn't realize he was being taken for a ride. Maybe her fiancé was indeed the source of the money Annabelle's mother had seemed concerned about that first day by the pool.

"Is something wrong?" Annabelle murmured for his ears only as he held out her chair.

"No."

"Then why are you looking at me as if I have horns?"

"For all I know," Clay whispered in her ear as she sat, "under all that hair, perhaps you do."

She snatched the white linen napkin from her plate and snapped it open over her lap as she whispered, "Are you actually admitting that you don't know everything?"

He couldn't suppress a smile as he took the seat to her left. "I refuse to incriminate myself, counselor."

She was a beauty, he allowed, admiring the graceful column of her neck, noticing how the yellow dress reflected the gold in her eyes. Too bad the woman couldn't be trusted. He glanced across the table, exasperated that the older couple was so immersed in each other. They clasped hands and exchanged words in lowered voices. At the light in his father's eyes, Clay experienced a pang of resentment toward the woman whose affection for his father was most likely artificial, or at best, short-lived.

Clay knew his father's endless string of affairs was a weak attempt to replace his mother, with whom Martin had been so in love. He felt sorry for his father because he himself wasn't immune to the occasional twinge of loneliness. On the other hand, he refused to add to his father's inevitable heartache by encouraging a marriage to yet another crafty fortune seeker. His gaze bounced back to the dark-haired enchantress who nibbled on the nail of her forefinger as she scrutinized the menu. Or would that be *two* crafty fortune-seekers?

Annabelle felt Clay's dark eyes on her, but refused to lift her gaze lest he see how nervous this entire situation made her. The aromatic, upscale restaurant, the romantic strains coming from the pianist, the pink lighting overhead—all of it a far cry from her typical rushed meals out with business associates. Having dinner with their lovebird parents just seemed too much like a double date. And Clay looked too handsome in a navy suit and a startlingly white shirt for her attention span, which seemed unbelievably short this evening. She'd read the menu at least three times and couldn't remember a single dish.

"Would you like wine?" he asked, forcing her to look at him.

His blue eyes seemed to claim her. "No, thank you." She wanted to keep her head as clear as possible.

"I called ahead and ordered a bottle of champagne," Martin announced with a beaming smile at Belle. "To celebrate."

Annabelle and Clay exchanged a split-second glance.

"Of course," Clay relented in a low voice.

A waiter came to take their orders—Annabelle settled on mahi-mahi—and a young hostess wheeled a bucket of iced champagne to their table. Dom Perignon. To Annabelle's ears, the sound of the bottle being uncorked was like a gunshot—an analogy not lost on her. The sparkling wine looked like liquid gold in her glass, the tiny bubbles a testament to the quality of the libation—a far cry from the carbonated grape juice her parents bought for celebrations.

She blinked back a sudden wall of tears and held her glass carefully, her resolve to protect her mother hardening.

Martin coughed lightly, and she realized he expected Clay to make a toast. Clay blinked, then slowly raised his glass. She could see he was struggling for something appropriate to say.

"To Martin and Belle," he said finally. "May they each get out of life what they so richly deserve."

His voice sounded cordial enough, but Annabelle picked up on the double entendre. Martin and Belle, on the other hand, were too giddy with their own togetherness to notice his lack of sincerity. They clinked crystal happily and drank deeply. When she touched her glass to Clay's, their gazes locked. The distrust she saw there mirrored her own misgivings. Neither one of them wanted to be here. She lifted her glass to her lips and as the delicious champagne fizzed over her tongue, Annabelle dearly wished they were toasting a more deserving occasion.

Martin beamed. "Only a few more days until Belle will be Mrs. Martin Castleberry."

Annabelle felt sick to her stomach, but managed a watery smile. "Mom, did you tell Martin the caterer is going to charge double for a rush job?"

He frowned slightly. "Double? That hardly seems fair."

"I know," Belle murmured, "but there was no way around it. And besides, think of all the money we saved on invitations."

Annabelle cleared her throat delicately. "You could postpone the ceremony by a mere two weeks—think of the money you'll save on the food."

Her mother gave her a sharp glance. "Two weeks?"

"Which would give you a few more days to iron out the prenuptial agreement," Clay added.

Belle shook her head. "But everyone is coming Saturday. Annabelle, your aunt Macey and cousin Lorie will be here. Not to mention Lucille and Hollis, Maris and Lawrence, Jennifer, Emily, Porter—"

"I know, Mom. Every living relative we have is converging on Atlanta." With great restraint, she kept from rolling her eyes. Her cousins just wanted to meet a movie star. And eat lobster bisque that would be twice as expensive as it should be. And harass Annabelle because she was still single.

Martin laughed. "My two sisters are going to love you, Belle. And of course they're always delighted for an excuse to see Clay again—they keep hoping to make the trip from Massachusetts someday for *his* wedding."

Annabelle shifted her gaze to Clay. His frown was quick and deep, indicating his doting aunts were destined for disappointment.

"About that prenuptial agreement," Clay said, looking at his father. "I spoke to your attorney today and he said he could meet with you tomorrow morning."

His father's brow darkened. "Belle and I don't want a prenuptial agreement."

"I agree with you," Annabelle said to Clay. "In fact, I'd be glad to meet with your attorney to discuss Mother's interests."

"I'll just bet you would," Clay muttered.

Annabelle frowned. "Do you want a prenup or not?"

"Of course I do. But there's no need for you to become involved. Dad's lawyer has drawn up these agreements before."

"I'm sure your father alone keeps him busy," she said through gritted teeth.

Martin stood and extended his hand to Belle. "Since the two of them are in the mood to argue, why don't you and I dance?"

"Gladly," Belle said, shooting Annabelle an annoyed look as she took Martin's hand.

Annabelle sipped her champagne as she watched the couple glide across the small dance floor performing complicated moves her own generation would never master. Her father had preferred the radio to the television, and when a favorite old tune would come over the old receiver that sat on top of the refrigerator, he would tug her aproned mother to the center of the kitchen floor and spin her around. They would look at each other as if nothing in the world mattered except their love. Her eyes brimmed with tears, but she bit her tongue hard to rein in her memories. How could her mother forget so easily?

"Is something wrong?" Clay asked.

Annabelle blinked and her laugh came out dry. "Only everything."

"Oh? Things not working out as you'd planned?"

She bristled at his mocking expression. "No, not exactly. How about for you?"

He sipped from his drink, his eyes never leaving hers. For a split second, she thought she saw desire flash in their depths. Heat crept up her cheeks.

"No," he said finally. "Not exactly."

"Ladies and gentlemen," a man's voice sounded. "If I could have your attention for just a moment."

Annabelle turned to see the pianist encompassing the seated diners with a broad smile. On the dance floor, Martin and Belle slowed their steps.

"We are honored this evening to have as our guest the legendary actor, Mr. Martin Castleberry, and to help him celebrate his recent engagement."

Under the spotlight, Belle and Martin beamed at the applause. Annabelle joined in half-heartedly, marveling at her mother's ease, while Clay sat stonily silent.

"Won't you join the happy couple in a celebratory dance?" the man invited the crowd.

The pianist struck up a slow, jazzy version of 'You Made Me Love You,' and sang in nostalgic tones, "I didn't wanna do it...."

Several couples left their tables to join Martin and Belle on the floor. She made eye contact with her mother, who waved for her and Clay to join them, prompting Martin to do the same to Clay. Annabelle felt tingly and uncomfortable, her body straining oddly toward the man who triggered a baffling response in her.

Clay seemed as exasperated as she when he stood and extended his hand. "Let's get this over with."

She wanted to turn him down, she really did. To watch the imposed-upon expression fall from his face. But heaven help her, the thought of moving around the dance floor in his arms wasn't entirely repugnant. In fact, her pulse jumped rather dramatically at the sight of his big body towering over her. He looked positively splendid in his immaculate suit and open-collared dress shirt.

"Yes, let's," she agreed with equal irritation, and rose to walk with him to the edge of the dance floor.

A dozen couples shared the small area, but Annabelle felt oddly singled out and conspicuous as Clay swept her into a slow waltz. His warm hands curved around her waist and clasped her hand in the air above her shoulder. The scent of his musky aftershave brought back the memory of his rough kiss the day he'd shown up at her mother's prepared for a showdown. Had it been only two days ago? For some strange reason, she felt more entwined with this man than their hours together might indicate.

The top of her head barely reached his shoulder, and he was easily twice her breadth. Not a small woman, Annabelle felt dwarfed by Clay's size. The sensations of feeling overwhelmed versus safe warred within her. Inches separated their bodies as they moved in a neat circle under his guidance. Since her father's passing, her dance steps had become rusty; Clay on the other hand, moved effortlessly. She concentrated fiercely to keep from stepping on his expensive shoes.

"Relax," he murmured, giving her the slightest of smiles.

"I'm out of practice," she said, hating how he could read her body language.

"Doesn't your boyfriend ever take you dancing?"

She missed a step and came down on his toes, not entirely by accident.

He recovered instantly, but his smile turned wry. "I guess not."

Annabelle pressed her lips together to suppress her own smile, then relaxed a fraction of an inch. Clay had no idea he was beginning to affect her—indeed, he thought she was engaged. She was completely safe.

Then she swallowed hard. So why was he *stroking* her back?

Squashing the desire stirring in her stomach, she told herself he was simply keeping time to the music as he swept her around. Nonetheless, his touch wasn't wholly objectionable.

"You made me love you," the singer crooned. "I didn't wanna do it...."

Clay was outrageously handsome, she acknowledged. His face was a collection of superb, masculine lines that would undoubtedly incite legions of female fans. And certainly the Castleberry name would have opened a few doors in Hollywood. "You were never interested in an acting career?"

His scoff was quick and hearty. "Never."

Although she suspected she was treading on dangerous territory, she asked, "Why not?"

He took his time answering, which gave her a legitimate reason to look into those bottomless blue eyes. A mistake, because it made her curious as to what was lingering behind them. Did the man still see her as a problem to be eliminated? Or had he graduated to plain indifference?

"Let's just say I saw what it did to my father's personal life, and I wanted no part of it."

Did Clay have a personal life, she wondered? A lover waiting for him in Paris? "So you can understand why I don't want my mother dragged into the spotlight."

His eyes narrowed slightly, then he turned to watch their parents. "They seem rather determined, don't they?"

A few feet away, the couple exchanged adoring looks as they moved together effortlessly.

Annabelle sighed. "Yes, they do. Maybe we should just give our blessing and get back to our own lives."

His fingers stroking her back stilled. "Why the sudden change of heart?" His voice sounded odd—almost suspicious.

She shrugged. "I don't know. I guess I'm thinking who am I to tell my mother she shouldn't marry."

"Especially since you're about to take the plunge yourself?" he asked lightly.

She opened her mouth to tell him the truth, but the interest in his expression frightened her. Why make herself more vulnerable to his charisma by telling the man that not only was she not engaged, she hadn't been on a bona fide date in eight months, three weeks, and four days.

She, Annabelle Garnet Coakley, was ripe for the picking.

"Well," she managed to say, "my situation is a bit different than my mother's."

"Oh? Your fiancé isn't a rich, older man?"

She averted her eyes. "No."

"Someone you work with?"

Annabelle missed another step. She'd told her share of little white lies for the greater good, but something about this man made her feel as if she were turned inside out for him to analyze. "I'd rather not discuss my personal life."

He arched one black eyebrow. "Careful—someone might think you're hiding something."

The man had radar like a bat. Swallowing hard, she said, "You seem determined to think the worst of me."

Seconds ticked by while he stared down at her with that unreadable half-smile. "On the contrary," he said finally. "Those freckles of yours are wreaking havoc with my better judgment."

Struck speechless, Annabelle missed another step. Suddenly, he spun them around in a move that forced their bodies together. She sucked in a sharp breath, dismayed at the thrill that pulsed through her as her breasts pressed into his chest. His arm bridled her waist, holding her against him, their legs moving intimately, like the blades of scissors.

She closed her eyes against the sensation of her body moving against his. Some small part of her said she should resist, should break free of his embrace, but his arms simply felt too good wrapped around her. And his words reverberated in her head. The fact that he found her attractive shocked her, but the fact that he would admit it flat out astonished her.

Annabelle had no time to consider the matter further because the singer wrapped up the song with a flourish. Near them, Martin lowered Belle into a dramatic dip, to enthusiastic applause. For their own end, Clay released her slowly. Annabelle didn't trust herself to make eye contact. She was afraid she might see an invitation lingering there, an invitation that would compromise her vow to avoid messy entanglements of dating, affairs or—horror of horrors—a relationship.

Not that someone like Clay Castleberry would ever embark on a relationship. At least not with her.

Alarmed at the shift in her awareness of the man next to her, she kept her eyes riveted on their parents, and noticed her mother was limping. Great—Martin wanted to show off his fancy schmancy moves and had managed to sprain her ankle, or throw out her back, or break her hip.

She rushed forward, ready to sweep her mother out of harm's way. "Mom, are you hurt?"

"Thank goodness, no," Belle said. "The heel to my sandal broke off." She held up the 3-inch wedge, laughing.

Relieved, Annabelle nonetheless shot Martin a reproachful look. "I'll take you home, Mother."

"Nonsense, Annabelle," Martin boomed. "I'll take your mother home to fetch another pair of shoes. You and Clay stay and enjoy yourselves—we'll be back before you know it."

Clay fished the valet ticket from his pocket, his movements hesitant.

Panic blipped in her chest at the thought of spending time alone with Clay and her gaze flew to his. Her reaction must have shown on her face because her mother whispered, "Remember your manners, dear."

Martin helped Belle to the table where she retrieved her purse and smiled graciously at onlookers before moving toward the exit. Annabelle stopped next to the table, feeling as if the situation was slipping out of her grasp.

With a start, she realized Clay had pulled out her chair and was patiently waiting for her to claim it. When she glanced up, a tight smile played on his handsome face.

"I suppose we have no choice but to endure each other's company for a while," she offered nervously, taking the seat.

He bent over, scooting her and her chair closer to the table, then whispered near her ear, "This could be interesting."

CHAPTER TEN

DINING ALONE WITH CLAY Castleberry, interesting? Nerve-wracking, disquieting, and downright uncomfortable, perhaps, but not interesting. Annabelle sipped her champagne and studied the man sitting next to her as he asked their waiter to bring appetizers and delay the entrees until their parents returned. Admittedly, he was an intriguing man. If they had met under different circumstances, would they have—

"Well?" he asked.

Annabelle jerked—darn it, caught daydreaming again. "Well, what?"

"Well, what now? I can see the wheels turning in your head. I assume you have a plan."

A guilty flush descended. How long would he gloat if he knew that her confusing attraction to him was distracting her from her main goal to…to… oh, yes—to stop the wedding.

She cleared her throat. "Short of kidnapping, I'm not certain what to do with my mother."

"We're running out of time," he said, his words measured.

Did she imagine it, or did his gaze flit to her ring finger? "Yes, we are. The more plans they make, the less chance we have of changing their minds."

Clay shook his head. "Women always manage to turn a simple ceremony into an overblown event."

Annabelle blinked. "May I point out that getting married isn't as old hat for my mother as it is for your father. Surely you can't begrudge her a few indulgences."

Clay rolled his eyes. "I suppose you're neck-deep into planning your own production."

Annabelle frowned, determined not to be distracted. "Don't you think a couple should be surrounded by their family and friends when they take their vows?"

"Since *no* marriage is likely to last, why inconvenience everyone else?"

She was torn—half in agreement, yet faintly dismayed that neither of them carried within them the belief they could find one person to love for all time. His cynicism was jarring, but hadn't she mouthed similar sentiments to everyone within earshot?

"Well, even if Mother goes ahead with this wedding," she murmured, "I'm glad she at least wanted me to be here and take part in the ceremony."

Clay gripped his glass as the unwitting barb hit home. Conversely, his father had gone out of his way to prevent him from finding out about the ceremony. He preferred to think his father was trying to get away with something rather than excluding his son from an important day in his life. He tossed back the last of his champagne. Surely their relationship had not deteriorated that badly.

He probed his cheek with his tongue, irritated to realize that he'd rather be exploring fantasies with the lovely engaged Annabelle than discussing the shortcomings of the Castleberry men. Still, things were what they were—she was off-limits, and their parents were off their rockers.

"It won't bother you," he asked, "being witness to a union you know is destined to fail?"

"Yes," she said, sliding her tongue over those wonderful lips. "But no matter what happens, I can't turn my back on my mother."

She looked earnest enough. But was it simply an act, to pretend she was being worn down when she was really fostering the marriage behind the scenes? The phone inside his jacket pocket vibrated. He pulled it out, half-hoping the call was from Paris and dire enough for him to return immediately.

Instead, it was his father reporting they'd driven Belle's car home and arrived safely, but now the car wouldn't start. They had opted to order in Chinese food and watch a video at Martin's, but why didn't Clay and Annabelle stay and have a nice dinner? They'd all catch up later, when Clay brought Annabelle home. Clay opened his mouth to say no, that they'd be right home, but stopped when he glanced across at Annabelle, her lips slightly parted, her eyebrows raised in question. Unbidden lust rolled through his body.

On the other hand, when might he have another chance to spend time with her one-on-one and discover something unpleasant to counteract the powerful attraction he felt when she cast those golden eyes in his direction?

"Sure thing, Dad. We'll see you soon."

He hung up slowly, scrutinizing his accidental companion for the evening. Had she felt the same stirring as he when he'd pulled her close on the dance floor? No, he decided. If the flash of interest he'd seen in her eyes was longing, she was thinking either about her fiancé, or about getting her graceful little hands on his father's estate.

Clay broke the news to her, keen for her reaction. She appeared to be at loss for a reason to decline, and her silent acquiescence coincided with the waiter delivering skewers of prosciutto and cantaloupe. With an apology, he canceled Martin and Belle's orders, then ordered another bottle of champagne, both to pacify the waiter, and to—hopefully—loosen her tongue.

She ate delicately, helping herself to a small portion of the appetizer. He was absurdly pleased when she smiled and nodded in approval at his choice. "Delicious," she said, dabbing at the corners of her mouth. "You're a wonderful dancer."

Taken off guard, he said, "It helps to have a good partner." Then he straightened. "Er, dance partner, that is."

She lifted an eyebrow. "Have you ever been married?"

He laughed without humor. "No."

A dubious look came over her face. "Not even a near miss?"

"No. No time or inclination." The waiter reappeared with more champagne and refilled their glasses.

"Hm. So tell me about your job."

Darn it, *he* was supposed to be asking the questions. “What do you want to know?”

She shrugged. “Describe your typical day.”

He felt stubbornly resistant to disclosing details of his life, personal or not. “There’s no such thing as a typical day, but I spend most of my time reviewing start-up companies and their products, then marrying them with an investor or group of investors.”

“You’re a glorified matchmaker?”

Clay frowned. “That’s one way of putting it, I suppose.”

“And do you ever invest in these companies?”

Was she trying to determine his earning power? “Sometimes,” he said carefully. “But my value comes more from having strategic contacts, and recognizing the right fit people-wise.” She popped a small section of melon into her mouth. He’d never known the simple act of chewing could be so provocative.

“So,” she said, angling her head at him. “In a way, you can tell if two people are right for each other.”

Clay balked. “Strictly in the business sense.”

She drank more champagne. “But isn’t marriage sort of like a business deal?”

In spite of wearing a collar-less shirt, he suddenly felt pretty hot around the collar. “I never thought about it.”

“What with prenuptial agreements, and vows, and community property laws.” She smiled. “Not to mention bribes.”

“I suppose there are some similarities.” Clay shifted in his seat, wondering how the heck the tables had turned.

“So, in a way, you *are* able to tell if two people are right for each other.”

“I don’t think—”

“Or at least *wrong* for each other?”

Clay swallowed hard. Her eyes shone, her skin was luminous. Was she still talking about their parents, or someone else? In an amazingly short period of time, Annabelle Coakley had mastered the uncanny ability to turn his thoughts inside out. They were even more wrong for each other than their parents...weren’t they?

Luckily their entrees arrived, suspending the line of questioning. Clay exhaled and tried to relax, but became irritated when the waiter lingered at Annabelle's elbow an inordinate amount of time, offering an array of unnecessary spices, condiments, and services. The transparent fellow, however, couldn't seem to take his eyes from her chest. Clay cleared his throat noisily and frowned at the young man, who quickly moved along. Pesky pup.

"Mmmm," Annabelle murmured after tasting the mahi-mahi. "This is incredible."

He closed his eyes, resisting the urge to tell her to keep her sounds of satisfaction to herself. Instead he asked, "So what's a typical work day for you?"

She chased the food with a quick sip from her glass, then lifted her slim shoulders in a shrug. "I meet with clients in the morning, then I'm in court all afternoon, then I do research in the evening."

An ambitious schedule, if she spoke the truth. "I hope you take weekends off."

She shook her head, dislodging a strand of dark hair that fell in front of her right ear. "I prepare for cases on the weekends."

"That doesn't leave much time to see your fiancé," he observed.

At her hesitation, he knew he'd hit a nerve. The woman *was* hiding something.

"Does your job require you to travel a great deal?" she asked.

He pretended not to notice the shift in subject. "I can control my schedule based on the projects I select. This year I've traveled quite a bit by choice." To avoid his father, he acknowledged silently.

"To avoid your father?"

Clay frowned. "Why do you say that?"

"Because it's obvious the two of you aren't close."

"We're different," he said with a shrug.

"My mother and I are different, but we're still close."

He didn't owe her an explanation, this virtual stranger. Especially since she might have ulterior motives. Still, he felt compelled to say, "My father wasn't around much when I was growing up."

"And now that you're grown, *you* aren't around much."

He bit down on the inside of his cheek. "Don't judge me."

"I'm not judging you," she added, holding up her hand. "Just making an observation based on my own experience. I left my mother alone, too, moved hundreds of miles away. You know, we only have ourselves to blame that they ended up in the arms of someone we don't approve of."

"We have to live our own lives," Clay said, unwilling to accept one iota of blame for his father's foolish behavior.

"Are you happy?" she asked, leaning forward on her elbows.

Clay realized from the glossy look in her eyes that she did not have a high tolerance for alcohol. And good champagne could be deceptively intoxicating to a small person on an empty stomach. Her tongue was getting loose, all right, but she was turning philosophical on him. "I, uh…yes...I'm happy."

"You don't seem happy."

Irritated, Clay frowned. "I'm happy, I tell you."

"I'm happy, too," she said quietly, her frown mirroring his, as if she was confused.

She started to take another drink from her glass, then set it down and pushed it away. Mesmerized by the emotions crossing her face, he watched her shake herself, sit upright, and turn her attention to her meal. Anyone could see an invisible shield had slid into place around her.

The strains of music and the buzz of conversation sounded all around them, but after a few minutes of silence, Clay missed the sound of her voice. He attempted to engage her into conversation, but her answers were monosyllabic and vague. Perturbed at her for her moodiness, and at himself for caring, he withdrew into his own thoughts, which, unfortunately, seemed to be dominated by his beautiful companion. He itched to dance with her again, to have an excuse to hold her close, but frankly, the woman spooked him. If she could get under his skin in a matter of days with his guard firmly in place, what damage might she wreak if given free rein? And he didn't like the kinds of thoughts she unleashed in his mind.

Happy? He scoffed—of course he was happy.

Clay ate quickly, but Annabelle pushed aside her plate even sooner and turned in her seat to watch the singer perform, her fingers drumming lightly on the tabletop. He memorized her tilted profile, feeling excluded, but more intrigued than on his last date with a woman who fawned over him all night, yammering until he was tempted to stuff the cork from the wine bottle into his ears.

But this woman…this woman captivated him.

Bewildered by his fixation on her, he flagged the waiter for the check, paid for dinner over Annabelle's protests, and shepherded her inside his car after the valet drove up to the sidewalk.

"Thank you for dinner," she said, fastening her seatbelt.

"You're welcome." He put the car into gear and pulled out onto the street. "You fell quiet in there all of a sudden."

Annabelle turned to stare out her window. "Sometimes I talk too much."

Clay pursed his mouth. Was she afraid she had almost revealed something damaging? He hoped Henry would find out something soon to either prove or disprove his suspicions that Annabelle Coakley was up to something.

They drove home in relative silence, although the interior of the car was filled up with her—her scent, her aura. Clay found himself leaning toward her, straining to hear the little sighs she uttered, to catch the rise and fall of her breasts. Worse, the tiny strap of her bra had fallen down her left shoulder a couple of inches—a strap he recognized. Knowing she was wearing the skimpy animal-print underwear had him smoldering.

Clay shifted restlessly, turning up the volume on the radio to waylay his libido. Darkness, he acknowledged, had a way of blinding a man to all the reasons he shouldn't be attracted to a woman, instead evoking images of delectable nighttime activities. By the time they neared their parents' neighborhood, he had worked himself into a state he hadn't known since his teenage years, when sex was new and exciting, before he'd experienced the emotional baggage that went along with becoming involved with a woman.

"Shall I drop you at your mother's house?" Clay asked.

"Drive on to your father's. I'll collect mother and take her home," she said as if she were snatching a child out of harm's way.

He had to hand it to her—she certainly acted as if she opposed this wedding. She was perhaps the most beautiful con woman he'd ever met.

When they entered his father's house, Martin waved to them from the den off the foyer. He was watching television alone, smoking a pipe. "Belle was tired and wanted to turn in early. How was dinner?"

Excruciating. Clay forced a tight smile and said, "Fine."

"Can I get you a drink, Annabelle?"

She declined. "I'd like to catch Mother before she goes to sleep."

"I'll drive you," Clay offered.

"Thanks, but I'll just use the path. Goodnight."

Clay watched her walk to the door, riveted to her legs, and acknowledged that he wasn't quite ready to end the evening. "I'll walk with you," he said, and exited with her, ignoring her protests.

He retrieved a flashlight from his car, then walked alongside Annabelle through the darkness as she picked her way along the side of the house until she came upon the faint, uneven path that led into the patch of woods between their parents' homes.

"You really know your way around here," he observed.

"I used to put out salt block for the deer where your father's swimming pool is," she said, her dry tone not lost on him.

He held aside low branches, the sticky June humidity seeping into his skin. Crickets and cicadas quieted, then resumed their song in waves as the crunch of their footsteps sounded in the night. Clay was struck by the fact that most women he knew wouldn't dream of traipsing through the woods in a nice dress and heels, but Annabelle seemed unfazed. The woman had potential, he conceded.

And a fiancé, his mind whispered.

Annabelle was all too aware of Clay moving through the woods next to her, even though she couldn't see him. In fact, with her vision hampered, her other senses seemed to heighten. She smelled his soap and cologne. She felt his big body displacing the foliage around her. She heard his footfalls, his steady breathing. Her nerves danced from Clayton Castleberry overload.

The man was simply too…too *much*. Too handsome, too intelligent, too moody, too confusing. Frankly, she couldn't wait to reach the safety of her mother's home. Spotting the backyard lights ahead, she picked up the pace, then promptly stepped into a hole, and fell flat on her back.

Hard. An unladylike "woof" escaped her as the breath was chased from her lungs.

Before she could inhale again, strong fingers circled her upper arms and pulled her to a sitting position. "Are you all right?" Clay asked, concern coloring his voice. The flashlight he'd abandoned lay on the path, fanning a fixed beam over her legs and feet.

"Just had the wind knocked out of me," she croaked, mortified.

"Can you stand?"

She nodded, then realized he couldn't see her, which was good because her back felt moist—her dress was surely ruined. "Yes," she mumbled.

He slowly pulled her to her feet, assuming her weight. When the absurdity of the situation struck her, a laugh bubbled out of her throat. In the darkness, the noise sounded strange even to her own ears, but under the circumstances, laughing was better than the alternative—crying.

Would this day never end?

To her immense relief, Clay's soft chuckle floated out to mingle with hers, which fueled her laughter further, weakening her limbs. She leaned into him, brushing at her dress, rubbing a tender spot on her hip. "Our parents have probably traveled this path a thousand times without mishap, and I almost come up lame."

Suddenly conscious of his proximity, she cleared her throat and tried to stand on her own. He shifted, and his face was thrown into relief from moonlight pushing past the trees above them. His dark eyes were crimped at the corners, shining with humor—a different look for him. And a good one. She emitted a small laugh. "This has not been the best of days."

His answering silence only made her more nervous, especially since he seemed slow in relinquishing his hold on her. *His hold on her.* She swallowed, trying to identify the sensation that hung in the air between them. Lust? Curiosity? Loneliness?

"Perhaps we can salvage what's left of the day," he whispered, and the light disappeared as his body eclipsed the moon.

She was ready when his lips found hers, ready to satisfy the unexplainable yearning she had come to associate with his presence, ready to move past this insane attraction and return to comfortable indifference. His mouth moved firm and eager upon hers, as if he, too, wanted to extinguish the mysterious heat between them. At first he held her loosely, but as his warm tongue sought hers, his hands splayed against her back, wedging her body against his.

She threaded her fingers into the thick hair at the nape of his neck. He moaned into her mouth, overriding the symphony of night sounds around them, sending her senses soaring. He tasted of sweet champagne, smelled of warm musk, and held her with restrained power emanating the length of his body. They plundered each other's mouth ruthlessly, seeking relief in—or perhaps *from*—the other.

Seconds evaporated, then minutes, and even though her lungs screamed for oxygen, she was unwilling to end the exhilarating kiss. But when his hands slid down over her hips, she was jarred back to reality—there was no sensible end to this madness.

She turned to pull out of his embrace, gasping for air, and wrapped her arms around herself. What was she thinking? Skulking around in the dark, *kissing*, when she should be trying to stop her mother's ill-fated wedding. Annabelle shook herself—had both of the Coakley women lost their minds?

"I should get back," she said, her voice echoing loudly in her ears.

After a few seconds' hesitation, he retrieved the flashlight and waved for her to precede him. She wished she could see his face, but she could only guess from his casual body language that the accidental encounter hadn't been nearly as earth shattering an experience for him. He shined the light in front of her feet as she walked, and although he maintained a respectable distance as they entered her mother's backyard, his fingers brushed her back twice, sending shooting reminders of their passionate kiss to her midsection. Fighting the urge to hurry lest she fall again, Annabelle picked her way carefully along the rock walkway she'd helped her father lay when she was fourteen.

When the motion detector light for the deck blinked on, Clay extinguished the flashlight. With her heart still thumping with latent desire, Annabelle dug in her tiny purse for the house key, half-anticipating, half-dreading a serious talk with her mother about their foolishness.

Er, their *parents'* foolishness, that is.

"Thanks for walking me home," she said hurriedly, hoping that, where Clay was concerned, out of sight would mean out of mind.

He averted his eyes and scratched his temple. "Annabelle, about what happened back there—"

"There's no need to apologize," she cut in.

A frown creased his brow. "I wasn't going to apologize."

Perturbed, Annabelle put one hand on the doorknob. "Just like you didn't apologize the first time?"

"No," he sputtered. "I mean…yes!"

Pretending the knob was his head, she twisted it hard and pushed open the door. Why she'd ever let the man kiss her, she didn't know. "*Good*night," she said through gritted teeth.

"What's so good about it?" he snapped.

"This." She stepped inside and slammed the door in his handsome, infuriating face. "Oooooh!" she muttered at the closed door, so tempted to make a demonstrative gesture. The man brought out the worst in her!

"And what was that all about?"

Annabelle whirled around and sheepishly faced her mother, who sat at the breakfast bar in her robe under the low glow of a nightlight, her hands around a mug, her eyebrows high.

"I, um…Clay walked me to the door."

Her mother sipped. "And you had words?"

Annabelle managed an off-hand smile and walked toward the bar. "It was nothing, really."

Her mother squinted. "What on earth happened to your dress?"

"I fell on the path between the Castleberry house and here."

Belle stood, instantly on Mom-alert. "Are you hurt?"

"No," she assured her quickly, leaning over to unbuckle the thin ankle straps of the silver sandals. "I only humiliated myself in front of Mr. Perfect." *In more ways than one.*

"Oh." Her mother walked around the counter, wearing a smile. "So that's why you sounded so defensive. Were the two of you civil long enough to at least have a nice dinner?"

Annabelle nodded, eager to change the subject. "Martin said you were going to turn in early—aren't you feeling well?"

"Just tired from all the excitement, I suppose, but I wasn't able to sleep." She held up her cup. "I thought a little warm milk might help. There's more in the pan, want some?"

Annabelle smiled, then opened an overhead kitchen cabinet. Her fingers lit upon her father's favorite coffee cup, a black mug that featured the words 'Love sustains, maintains, and above all, remains.' Taking the coincidence as a sign, she removed the mug and held it out for her mother to fill with milk. Belle hesitated for half a second when she saw the cup, but poured without comment from the still-warm pan. "Vanilla?"

Annabelle nodded, comforted by the familiar routine of her mother adding a few drops of pure vanilla to the mug. "Just like old times," she murmured.

A fond smile crossed Belle's face, then she winked. "Except I use skim milk now. Your father always insisted on whole."

Annabelle swallowed the quick rush of tears with her first sip of flavored milk. "You never seemed to mind his little idiosyncrasies."

"Your father felt loved when he was being taken care of."

"You were so good at taking care of us, Mom."

Her mother reached out to stroke her hair that had escaped the clasp when she fell. "I wanted to make the two of you happy."

To make *them* happy? It had never occurred to Annabelle that her mother hadn't enjoyed every single minute of being a housewife. Trying to steer the conversation toward the topic uppermost in her mind, she said, "Right now I'd be very happy to hear you say you'll reconsider marrying Melvin Castleberry."

"It's 'Martin,' dear, and we're very much in love."

"Mom, how can you be in love with someone in such a short amount of time?"

Belle adopted an indulgent expression. "I can't explain it, but I *can* tell you it was the same with me and your father."

Annabelle chewed on her lower lip. It was a hard point to argue, considering her parents had been happily married for over thirty years. "Times have changed."

But her mother only laughed. "Not so much, dear. Falling in love hasn't changed over the ages. You'll see." She gestured in the air with animation. "One day you're going through life and everything seems perfectly ordinary, and then you stumble across a person who makes you feel so *alive*!" She sighed, beaming.

Annabelle shook her head, mostly to banish the unbidden image of Clay's face in her mind. "You sound like Mike. I'm sorry, but I see enough broken marriages every day to give me a slightly different perspective."

Her mother sipped her milk and pointed her pinkie. "I know, which is why I'm being patient with your meddling."

Annabelle gaped. "Meddling?"

"Uh-hm. You and Clay both. All your talk about prenuptial agreements and such."

She set down her mug. "Mom, Clay and I are the only people around here making sense!"

Belle raised an eyebrow. "You and the man you just slammed the door on?"

Annabelle frowned. "He's difficult."

"So are you, sometimes. But—" Her mother held up her hand. "I know you're only saying these things because you care about me."

"That much is true. I don't think I'm going to change my mind about this wedding, Mom."

Belle gave her a little smile. "And I don't think I'm going to change my mind, either." She nodded toward the door. "How about if we continue this discussion with our milk in my bedroom?" She smiled. "Just like old times."

Feeling a rush of love, Annabelle picked up her cup and draped her other arm around her mother's waist. "Just like old times. Let me change out of this soiled dress, and I'll be right in."

"Oh, by the way, dear, Martin and I are going hiking on Mt. Paxton tomorrow and taking a picnic."

Hiking? Her mother had never joined her and her father on their occasional hiking trips. Then she frowned into her milk—they had invited her, hadn't they?

"And we were hoping that you and Clay would join us."

Annabelle's heart fell to her stomach. A full day in the company of Clay Castleberry? "But I thought you and I were going to spend every moment together before the—you know." Else how was she going to convince her mother in the scant days left that marrying Martin was a bad idea?

"It's my and Martin's two-month anniversary, and we want to celebrate with a picnic."

Annabelle glanced down at her bare feet. "I didn't exactly bring the right shoes for hiking."

"There's a box of your things in the attic, and I'll bet you'll find those old boots of yours. It'll be fun and give us all another chance to get to know each other better since I messed up our dinner plans. Please, dear?"

Please. How could she refuse when her mother looked like a hopeful child? Annabelle conjured up a smile. "For you, Mom, of course I'll go."

She padded to her bedroom and changed quickly, baffled by the spring in her step. Why would she be anticipating another almost certain run-in with Clay? Pushing the troubling thoughts from her mind, she shrugged into a robe, then walked down the hall to her mother's room, only to find Belle fast asleep on top of the comforter.

Annabelle smiled, then covered her mother with a cotton afghan. She finished her lukewarm vanilla milk in her own bedroom, sitting in a chair next to the window. Her eyes kept gravitating to a lone light near the top of the Castleberry house. Was Clay still awake? If he was, she chastised herself, he wasn't sitting in a chair thinking about her, unless he was plotting her demise.

She bit down hard on the inside of her cheek. Why did she find this man so infuriating, so intriguing, and so…desirable? It was his energy, she realized, that made him different than any man she'd ever known. Brooding? Yes. Opinionated? Yes. Successful? Absolutely. But incredibly, exceedingly, and indubitably stimulating, both to her mind and her body.

One day you're going through life and everything seems perfectly ordinary, and then you stumble across a person who makes you feel so alive….

Annabelle frowned at her mother's words. She was not falling for Clay Castleberry. She simply wouldn't let herself.

CHAPTER ELEVEN

HOW WAS IT POSSIBLE, Clay asked himself, that the woman could look more distracting wearing khaki shorts, bulky socks, and clubby hiking boots than in the bathing suit she'd worn the other day? He hadn't been keen on hiking with the Coakleys when his father had suggested it first thing this morning, and upon seeing Annabelle, the merits of the idea continued to erode.

"A smile would be nice," his father said, elbowing him. "Belle and I both wish you kids would make an effort to get along."

Clay chewed on the inside of his cheek, the slam of the Coakley door still ringing in his ears. And the memory of that damned kiss had kept him awake, flipping through financial reports, unseeing, until the wee hours. He hoped Henry would furnish him with proof of the woman's intentions soon. Then he'd send Annabelle Coakley packing back to Michigan, minus any ill-gotten gains. "No offense, Dad, but she's not my first choice for female company."

His father frowned.

"But for your sake," Clay added with forced cheer, "I'll be nice."

His father's broad smile made his heart lurch—when had he become so easy to please? Clay pondered the revelation until he was distracted by Annabelle bending over to secure a boot lace. How, he wondered, could he make the most of this inconvenient outing?

An idea occurred to him, triggering a smirk. So she wanted him to believe she was against this marriage, huh? Okay, he'd force her to demonstrate her opposition.

"Annabelle," he called, walking over as she rose from her task at the end of his father's driveway. Her face was flushed from bending over, and she'd pulled her hair back into a high ponytail. With the freckles, she looked all of seventeen. Clay suddenly felt old.

And cranky.

"Yes?" She asked, raising her golden gaze to his. From the expression on her face, she was looking forward to the day almost as much as he.

Clay nodded toward the house. "Would you mind giving me a hand with the camera equipment?"

She glanced to where their parents were loading food into the back of Martin's sport utility vehicle, as if she wanted witnesses, then moved hesitantly toward the house.

As he followed her, he decided she must hit the gym pretty hard to keep her figure, and averted his eyes. "Do you hike a lot in Detroit?" he asked as he held open the door.

"Actually, I haven't been hiking since college. My dad and I used to go when I came home on semester breaks."

In the midst of their awkwardness, her words struck him—he'd almost forgotten they had something in common, losing a parent. Contrite, he gentled his voice. "Sounds fun. You must miss him."

She hesitated, then offered up a sad smile. "Enormously," she said as she walked by.

He followed her into the foyer, stopping next to a table where his camera bag sat. He chuckled to lighten the mood. "I asked because I was wondering if I'd be the only one with sore leg muscles—sometimes I can barely keep up with Dad when we run."

"I walk to work, and my office is on the twelfth floor." She smiled. "I manage to get in my workout without a gym."

Which explained her magnificent legs. Good girl—he preferred clearing the land he owned north of the city to working out at a gym.

"Where's the rest of your equipment?" she asked, peering around the entryway that was large enough for a room itself.

"This is it," he said, picking up the small bag. "It was an excuse to talk to you alone."

Her face reddened. "If this is about last night—"

"Annabelle, are you truly opposed to marriage?"

She blinked.

Clay caught his gaffe—the woman was engaged, after all. "I mean, *this* marriage."

"You know I am." She fidgeted, tucking a loose strand of shiny hair back into the clasp.

He studied her face for insincerity, but was sidetracked by her cheekbones. He adjusted the strap on the camera bag, trying to sound casual. "Then maybe we can work together today and put a stop to this wedding nonsense once and for all."

She crossed her arms and considered him for a few seconds. "I'm listening."

"Why do you suppose our parents are so determined to be married?"

Her demeanor changed immediately. She scratched, she shifted, she squirmed. "I wouldn't know."

Clay smirked. "Give me your best guess, counselor."

She studied the toes of her boots. "Well, they're probably caught up in all the tingly, romantic nonsense that goes along with being engaged, you know what I mean."

"No," he said, amused. "I've never been engaged."

"Well, surely you can *imagine* what my mother and your father are feeling." She gestured vaguely in the air.

"*Think* they're feeling," he corrected.

She nodded. "From my experience with clients—"

"And your own engagement," he reminded her.

"—most people don't plan past the honeymoon. But reality sets in when it gets down to dirty socks and what's for dinner."

Having never contemplated marriage, he hadn't given much thought to a honeymoon or dirty socks. Anxious for firmer footing, he squared his shoulders. "So today we'll simply take every opportunity to remind our parents that marriage isn't what it's cracked up to be. Of course," he added wryly, "you might come across as less than convincing since you yourself are engaged."

Annabelle paled slightly. "I'd rather you not mention my engagement."

He was instantly alert. "Why?"

"Because...I haven't told my mother yet."

Intrigued, he cocked his head. "Why not?"

"Because...this came up...and I didn't want to...muddy the waters."

Something wasn't right, he could feel it. Clay wished like hell he could read her mind. One thing was certain—he was more convinced than ever that Annabelle wanted to see her mother marry his father. But if she wanted to pretend otherwise, he'd make the most of it.

A frown marred her smooth forehead—she was probably realizing the corner she'd painted herself into. "I'll go along with your plan," she said, her tone cautious. "But I don't want my mother's feelings hurt."

"Likewise," he agreed. "If we team up, maybe they'll come to their senses."

A dubious look crossed her face, but she shrugged her acquiescence. "It couldn't hurt, I suppose." The same stubborn strand of hair slipped out of her ponytail and hooked around her cheek. The sun slanted in through the stained glass transom over the front door and highlighted the delicate angles of her face. She had a way of tightening her mouth when she was anxious that summoned her high dimples. This woman was a paradox. With her flaxen eyes, she looked catlike, with the potential of being lethal one moment, kittenish the next.

Which would he prefer? Out of the blue, the thought hit Clay between the eyes and he exhaled abruptly, realizing the day might very well require more endurance on his part than strong leg muscles.

Annabelle stopped to shift the equipment on her shoulders, frowning at the backs of Belle and Martin several yards ahead of her on the rocky trail. Even weighted down with a backpack, her mother moved like a nimble mountain goat. Meanwhile, *she* had a boulder in her left shoe and a bug bite just high enough on the back of her thigh to be unscratchable in mixed company.

"Need to rest?"

At the sound of Clay's amused voice, she looked over her shoulder and pursed her mouth. She wasn't sure what bothered her most—the fact that she couldn't keep up with her mother, or the fact that Clay's rear position on the single-file trail afforded him the opportunity to scrutinize every inch of her, unobserved.

Assuming he was inclined to look, that is.

"No." The word slipped out more tartly than she'd planned, so she tried again. After all, they were supposed to be working together. "No, I don't need to rest, thank you." She stopped and waited for him to climb closer. "I thought we were going to talk to them."

He wiped perspiration from his brow with the back of his hand. "We have to catch them first."

"If you hadn't yakked on your phone the entire drive up here," she accused, "we might've already made some headway."

One dark eyebrow lifted. "What, you can't talk without me?"

She jammed her hands on her hips, nearly throwing herself off balance with the heavy backpack. "Try to talk over you and the big band music they were listening to in the front seat, *and* be casual about the fact that this marriage is a dead end street."

He propped one foot on a stump and leaned on his knee, slapping a streak of dried red mud from his navy canvas shorts. His legs were thick with muscle and covered with dark hair. Standing next to Clay, she felt diminutive. Her neck warmed because she knew she looked a fright. Her ponytail clasp hung loose, a tree branch had torn the sleeve of her white T-shirt, and the stripe of pink zinc oxide on her nose, while smart, she knew wasn't exactly attractive.

Not that she was trying to be attractive.

"I presumed your job required you to be sly and persuasive," he said, but the cynical gleam in his eyes squashed any hint of a compliment.

"No more than your job, I suppose," she said, matching his tone.

"And are you good at your job?" he asked, surprising her.

"Good?"

"Squeezing lucrative settlements out of inattentive husbands?"

Anger sparked in her stomach, then quickly caught flame. She lifted her chin. "For your information, most of my clients do well to get child support, and I haven't handled a case yet where the marriage failed from lack of attention." She scoffed. "Besides, you act as if I receive a percentage of the settlements."

"You don't?"

In one glance, she took in the distinctive sunglasses tucked in the neck of his pale blue T-shirt, the hand-tooled leather waist pouch, the worn, but expensive lace-up boots—Clay Castleberry had always enjoyed a pampered lifestyle, and he was questioning *her* financial motives?

Her body sang with anger as she perused over six feet of unadulterated arrogance. Men! Her mother actually wanted to marry one of these? "My fiscal status is none of your business."

She'd been known to make men flinch in the courtroom with that tone, but Clay stood as still as the pine trees around him, an innocent smile on his lips. His shrug was a mere ripple of shoulder muscles. "I was simply trying to figure out why an attorney would steal underwear."

Annabelle looked around for something to gouge him with, but was interrupted by Martin's voice ringing out above them.

"Are you two slowpokes ready to stop for lunch?"

She looked up to the tree-studded ridge, but their parents had already disappeared around a rock formation. Annabelle huffed and swatted furiously at a fat bee, then set her sights on the incline before her. But when she took a hurried step forward, the offending pebble in her shoe jabbed the tender ball of her foot. She yelped, lurching sideways.

Powerful hands encircled her arm and waist from behind before she hit the ground, and her momentary pain relief was overridden by the realization that Clay was holding her, and the now-familiar sensation wasn't wholly unwelcome. Just unsettling.

"I'm going to start thinking you fall just so you can lean on me," he said in her ear.

His words rankled her, but his tone sent a thrill up the back of her neck. "I've learned not to lean on anyone," she said fastidiously, determined there wouldn't be a repeat of last night's lapse, no matter how tempting.

"Did you twist your ankle?" Clay asked, slowly righting her, but maintaining his grip. He sounded almost concerned as he lowered her to sit on the stump.

Though tempted to milk the situation as he molded his hands around her ankle, her conscience kicked in. "It's just a rock in my shoe."

He frowned and plucked at her thick brown sock that bagged around the top of her boot. "How did a rock get inside?"

"It must have been in my boot when I put it on, and I didn't notice." At the moment, all she noticed was that his eyes in the sunlight were the shade of blue that belonged in a television commercial selling diet soda. Or jeans. Or ice to an Eskimo.

Clay fumbled with the laces on her boot. She watched numbly as he loosened the boot from her leg and freed her foot. She wriggled her warm toes as he upended her boot to shake the rock into his hand.

"Did you lose a button?"

Annabelle frowned, then reached for the item he held out. But when the little pewter button bounced into her palm, she inhaled sharply. Memories assailed her, blurring her vision. Tears spilled over before she could gather herself.

"What's wrong?" Alarm rang clear in Clay's voice. He covered her knee with his hand. "Annabelle? What is it?"

She bit her lip to stem the tears, but her chin wouldn't stop quivering.

"Annabelle." She lifted her gaze to see genuine fear in his expression. "For God's sake, tell me."

She sniffed mightily, then touched the button stamped 'U.S. Army' with the tip of her finger and tried to smile. "It's from a vest my dad used to wear." His favorite item of clothing, a flak vest left over from his stint in the military as a young man. Tattered olive green with baggy pouches that held his favorite pocketknife, his best fishing lures, and the stash of hard candy he loved to share.

The image of her gray-haired, broad-shouldered father wearing the vest stood out in her mind as clearly as if he were standing next to her. *What do you say we go tease the trout in Johns Creek, Anna?*

She closed her fist around the button and pressed her knuckles to her mouth. How had the tiny disc found its way into her boot, and what was she to make of the timing of its discovery? It was as if the button were a sign, a reminder of her promise to her father.

"You must have been very close to him," Clay said, his voice surprisingly gentle.

She nodded, unable to look up. "We used to talk several times a week about a case I was studying or politics or…nothing at all." A sigh escaped her and she lifted her head. "Sometimes I forget he's gone and pick up the phone to call him."

He made a sympathetic sound, and removed a monogrammed handkerchief from his back pocket. "Here." Relief that he wasn't laughing at her quickly evaporated when she remembered Belle saying that Clay's mother had died when he was very young.

"Do you remember your mother?" she ventured as she wiped her cheeks, almost breathless to breach such a personal boundary. The songbirds in the branches above them suddenly seemed very loud.

Clay scooped a pinecone from the ground and ran his thumb down the side. "Yes. Although I've looked at her pictures so often, sometimes I wonder if I just remember the poses."

Her heart cracked for the little dark-haired boy who must have adored his glamorous mother. "How old were you when she died?"

He drew back his arm and casually tossed the pinecone into the woods, and for a few seconds she thought he wasn't going to answer. Then he looked back to her, his face impassive. "I was nine. My mother had several miscarriages after she gave birth to me, and she was thrilled to finally carry another baby to full-term. But the delivery was complicated, and she died."

"What—" Annabelle swallowed. "What about the baby?"

"Stillborn. A girl."

She pressed her lips together. "Oh, Clay, I'm so sorry."

He gave her a sad smile. "It was a long time ago."

"Your father must have been devastated."

Clay nodded. "Honestly, I don't think he ever truly recovered." A frown pulled at the corners of his mouth. "Hence the parade of women through his life."

And his son's, she realized, who'd had to share his father's attention when he'd needed him most. Resentment ballooned in her stomach toward Martin, reinforcing her opinion that he wasn't the kind of man to whom she would entrust her mother.

"Clay?" Martin's voice rang out. "Is everything okay?"

Speak of the devil. Annabelle scowled.

"We'll be right there," she and Clay yelled in unison, then looked at each other and smiled awkwardly.

Glad for the lighter moment, Annabelle bent to reclaim her boot and promptly banged heads with Clay—hard. She moaned and lifted a hand to explore the onset of a knot.

"Sorry," he said, laughing and massaging his own forehead.

"Just a reminder of how hard-headed we both are," she offered, managing a smile through the pain.

"I'll take care of your boot," Clay said, waiting for her slight nod before he knelt again. Her breath came in shallow little gulps as he held open the thick-soled boot and slipped her foot inside as gently as if he held a glass slipper. He rested her foot on his thigh, his knee to the ground, and methodically drew up the gold-colored laces. Her heart hammered as she watched his fingers, wide and blunt-tipped, securing the ankle-high boot. This man puzzled her—one minute she disliked him, and the next she...she....

"There," he said, patting her boot. He met her gaze and gave her a little smile that made her heart jerk. "Wow, you're going to have a goose egg," he said, lifting his hand to her forehead.

Struck silent by the electricity of his touch, she could barely breathe. A second later, his eyes changed from rueful to regretful, an odd expression on which to lean forward and claim a kiss, she thought fleetingly.

CHAPTER TWELVE

ANNABELLE CLOSED HER EYES a split second before his mouth descended on hers. The salt of perspiration, the warmth of sunned skin, the sweetness of surprise mingled on her tongue, and she reveled in the familiar textures of his mouth. He had controlled the first kiss, they had shared the second kiss, but she took possession of this one, coaxing him closer and deeper with her tongue. He came willingly, his lips firm and responsive, following her cues. A surge of female power gave her the energy to loop her arms around his neck. In answer, Clay's hands slipped to her waist, but he held her loosely, as if she might break.

The kiss took on a life of its own, gaining momentum and transferring pent-up frustrations and desires and emotions that were foreign to Annabelle. She strained against him blindly, not knowing what she wanted, only that she wanted more. But through the swirl of red passion, a rustling sound reached her ears. She stiffened and Clay drew away, swinging his head toward the noise on the path behind them.

Her gaze flew to the rise where her parents had vanished—what if they'd seen the kiss? After scanning the ridge, she sighed in relief, but her face burned from the near-miss. What was she thinking? How credible of an advisor could she be for her mother if she was indulging in stolen kisses with a man she barely knew—or liked, for that matter. Annabelle's mind spun—she had to get herself together.

Meanwhile, below them, a thin man with binoculars around his neck came into view. His safari-style hat and handheld guide identified him as a bird watcher. He waved with animation. Clay stood and pulled Annabelle to her feet, his expression perturbed.

"The trail's not too crowded today," the man observed with a tip of his hat as he passed them.

"Speak for yourself," Clay muttered at the man's back.

Annabelle laughed behind her hand, allowing herself to wonder where the kiss would have led if not for the timely interruption. She tingled under Clay's scrutiny, sensing he was just as confused by their kisses as she was. "Annabelle, I—"

"We'd better get going," she cut in, swallowing hard. "We still have a job to do."

He pursed his mouth and considered her for a few seconds, his gaze lingering on her lips before moving on. Then he simply nodded, and gestured for her to precede him on the path.

She exhaled and straightened her clothing unnecessarily, then marched ahead of him with as much dignity as she could salvage. Her wantonness shamed her. With every step up the dusty red clay path, she chastised herself. *Clay Castleberry tried to buy you off, remember?*

The man represented most of the things in life she railed against—entitlement, arrogance, superiority. *He doesn't think your mother is good enough to marry his father, but he thinks you're good enough to trifle with. He thinks you're engaged, for goodness sake.*

Her world was a cramped office on the twelfth floor of a state building in Detroit, Michigan. How foolish to expose her heart to a rich globe-trotter. *He mocked your measly state job—he'd never understand the satisfaction it gives you, helping women balance the scales against oppressive spouses.*

Annabelle picked up the pace, digging her boots into the sandy soil, eating up the ground between them and their parents. Clay's footsteps crunched behind her, but she tried to squash the awareness of him skittering over her arms. She'd marveled over the gullibility of her mother, yet scant minutes ago she'd allowed tingly feelings and base attraction to compromise her own self-respect.

Grasping the trunk of a tree to leverage herself, she stepped up on the rocky ridge and followed the narrow footpath around an enormous boulder. A few yards down the trail, the natural stone wall beneath her left hand led to a plateau, a sparsely wooded area off the trail, heavily carpeted with pine straw and dotted with picnic tables. Martin and Belle leaned against one, kissing.

Anna, promise me you'll look after your mother if something happens to me.

"Hi, Mom," she yelled through cupped hands, effectively distracting the older couple. She waved with enthusiasm and hurried over to the table on which their picnic lunch was already spread.

Clay watched Annabelle walk across the clearing, irritated that he had folded under her kiss, especially since he still didn't trust her. If he were going to get Martin out of this mess and return to his own business concerns in Paris, he'd have to keep a clear head. And that meant reverting to his previous plan to join forces with Annabelle *only* to dissuade their parents from marrying.

"What took you so long, dear?" Belle asked, casting an anxious glance over both of them. She probably thought they were arguing, he realized. If she only knew.

"Remember that flak vest Daddy used to wear?" Annabelle asked, her voice breezy.

Belle stopped, her full attention on her daughter. "Of course."

She held up the button. "Look what was in the bottom of my boot. How do you suppose it got there?"

As her mother took the button, Clay found himself studying Annabelle. Was the entire incident a setup? If so, what could the women possibly hope to gain? And deep in his heart he didn't want to believe that Annabelle would stoop to using the memory of her father as some kind of a ploy.

"It must have fallen off his vest and into your boot when I was packing away those things," Belle murmured, seemingly far away.

"This place is beautiful." Pink-nosed Annabelle changed the subject abruptly, lifting her arms and turning in a circle, encompassing the green, moist landscape. Using her phone, she snapped several photos of the incredible view, a few of Belle and Martin, and to his chagrin, one of him.

Clay squirmed. Never at ease in front of a camera, he was especially unnerved at the idea of Annabelle having a photo of him—it seemed familiar and *intimate*. Then he chastised himself for reading too much into a simple gesture—one might think he was projecting his own muddled feelings onto the woman.

Meanwhile, Annabelle put one arm around Belle's shoulder, and the other around Martin's shoulder. "Thank you for inviting us to come along. I'm having a great time." She gave him a pointed look.

Clay narrowed his eyes—what a little chameleon she was. Following her lead, he nodded his agreement. Actually, he *was* enjoying himself more than he'd expected. It was the fresh air, he reasoned. Invigorating.

"In fact, I think you should continue to celebrate your anniversary every month even after you're married." Annabelle kissed her mother's cheek, then took a seat at the table.

Clay bit down on his cheek. Where was this headed?

"We just might," Martin said, winking at Belle, then he leaned over to snatch a pickle from a vegetable-laden paper plate.

"With the failure rate of repeat marriages," Annabelle continued in a casual tone, "it's probably best to take it a month at a time." She plucked a celery stick from the plate and bit into it, snapping off the end with gusto.

Clay suppressed a smile, shed his own backpack and removed a bottle of water. "She's right," he added. "You two were smart to set a precedent of celebrating every month—so many couples never even reach their one-year anniversary."

At the wary exchange of glances between Martin and Belle, he knew they had struck a nerve, so he kept talking. "Was that your idea, Dad?"

Belle's gaze was glued on Martin. "Yes," she answered for him, her tone tinged with suspicion.

"Ah, that makes sense," Clay said to Annabelle as he swung his leg over the bench seat next to Martin, opposite his accomplice. "Because Dad's last four marriages didn't make it to the one-year mark."

Annabelle made a sympathetic noise, then swept her gaze over the food-laden table. "Whew, I'm starved."

"My stomach has been growling for the last two miles," Clay chimed in, then unwrapped the sandwich on the plate in front of him and lifted the top piece of crusty bread to appraise the filling. "Why is it everything tastes better in the outdoors?" He addressed their parents, but Belle still stared at his father, unsmiling.

"Everything Belle prepares is a delight," Martin boasted, oblivious to the tense undercurrents. "She's a wonderful cook."

Annabelle nodded her agreement, swallowing. "So, Martin, you expect Mom to cook, what—three meals a day?"

Clay chewed a bite of his roast turkey club. Surely his dad was smart enough to dodge *that* land mine.

"Of course not," Martin said, patting Belle's hand. "Two meals a day will suit me fine."

Clay winced. Belle shot Martin a sharp glance.

"Well, you're right about Mom's cooking," Annabelle said, licking mustard from her finger. "Has she made you her special fried pork chops with biscuits and gravy?"

Martin nodded, moaning in appreciation, which elicited a forgiving smile from Belle.

Clay took a long drink of water, studying Annabelle. For someone who was trying to get to his father's money, she was doing a good job of sabotaging the engagement. Could he have been wrong? Could Henry have been mistaken? A blow to his shin beneath the table took his breath, and he nearly choked. Annabelle's eyes widened meaningfully, and he realized she expected him to jump in.

"Um, Dad, didn't you tell your agent you'd drop ten pounds by Labor Day to emcee that fitness award show?"

Martin's hand stopped, a deviled egg halfway to his mouth, and looked down at his midsection. "You're right, son, I did." He returned the fattening morsel to his plate, and gave Belle an apologetic look. "Perhaps you *could* start cooking lighter meals. It would be good for both of us, Belle."

Annabelle gasped. "You think my mom is fat? I think she looks fabulous, don't you, Clay?"

At the bewildered look on his father's face, Clay almost felt sorry for him, but he reminded himself he had Martin's best interests at heart. "Yeah, Dad, Belle looks great. I don't know what you're talking about."

Belle stood abruptly, her expression hurt. "I'm not twenty-one, Martin."

Martin jumped to his feet. "I know you're not twenty-one! If I'd wanted a twenty-one-year-old—"

"Again," Annabelle injected.

"—again," he repeated involuntarily, "I would've proposed to a twenty-one-year-old!"

"Again?" Belle asked, leaned forward to plant her hands on the table. "And just exactly when *was* the last time you dated a twenty-one-year-old?"

"Wasn't Barbie twenty-one?" Clay asked his father, then removed the tomato from his sandwich. She was the last lover Clay had bought off.

"No!" Martin thundered. "She was twenty-five!"

"*Who* is Barbie?" Belle demanded.

"She's no one," Martin hurried to explain. "Just a girl who had a crush on me…a long time ago."

"For shame, Martin," Belle said, crossing her arms. "That's younger than my own daughter!"

"But I didn't marry her!"

Clay watched the drama unfolding, unable to believe that a few well-placed statements could have triggered such bedlam. Across the table, Annabelle quirked one eyebrow in triumph and chewed her food slowly.

He swallowed. The woman was frighteningly good at manipulation—there was a lesson to be learned here.

"Did the girl sign a prenuptial agreement?" Annabelle whispered loudly to Clay, although the comment was clearly meant to be overhead.

"No," he replied, which was true because she'd taken the pay-off money and disappeared.

Belle's jaw fell and she glared at Martin. "Is that why you're picking a fight? Because I haven't signed a prenuptial agreement?"

"Of course not!" Martin thundered.

"Have the papers drawn up," Belle declared. "I'll have Annabelle take a look at them and make sure I'm not being taken advantage of."

Clay cleared his throat. "But how could you be taken advantage of if the money belongs to my father?"

"My mother has assets of her own," Annabelle said, standing and planting her hands on the table in front of him.

Clay stood and leaned toward her. "The situation is hardly comparable."

Annabelle's mouth tightened. "Mom," she said, not taking her eyes off him, "the first day I met Clay—"

"Annabelle—" he warned, shaking his head.

"—he thought *I* was Martin's fiancée, and he offered me twenty thousand dollars to walk away."

"Clay," Martin admonished. "You didn't!"

Clay shifted his gaze to his father. "You know it wouldn't have been the first time I've had to pay off a woman for you, Dad."

"Martin!" Belle cried. "Is that true?"

While his father fumbled for an answer, Annabelle crossed her arms and donned a satisfied smile. "Clay told me Martin *expected* him to make the offer to get him off the hook of marrying you."

"I think it's time to go home," Belle said, her voice tremulous. She began shoving food into containers. A deviled egg slid across the table and rolled off, plopping onto the ground.

Martin put his fingers to his temples. "Would somebody tell me what just happened?"

"Dad," Clay said quietly, then made a cutting motion with his hand.

"I'll help you, Mom," Annabelle said, making comforting sounds as she joined her. Martin walked away from the picnic table, shaking his head. Clay looked at his sandwich with longing, then begrudgingly re-wrapped it and shoved it into his backpack.

His father stood with one hand leaning against a sycamore tree, staring out over the valleys of northern Georgia, the hues of green hinting at the distances—hunter, evergreen, olive, emerald, pistachio. Martin's head was down, reminding Clay of a little boy, and the irony of the child becoming the parent swept over him. His father's sadness always shook him—he remembered the ghastly weeks following his mother's and baby sister's funerals. Only the knowledge that his father's heart was resilient and his affection for Belle temporary kept Clay from feeling morose for the current situation.

"Great place," he observed, filling his lungs with pine-scented air.

Martin remained silent and Clay was startled to see his eyes were unusually moist. A blink later, the sheen was gone. "Your mother and I used to come up here."

Clay's heart squeezed. "I didn't know that."

"We brought you once or twice, but you were small." Martin laughed suddenly. "Delia wouldn't even put you down for fear you would run off the edge of some cliff."

"I don't have clear memories of Atlanta until just before she died," Clay admitted.

His father turned back to the view. "The two of you were with me most of the time in Los Angeles. When she became pregnant the last time, she wanted to come back home to Atlanta and be with her mother, and I agreed. By that time I was tiring of L.A. myself, so I sold the house there and secured an apartment to work out of, then commuted back and forth to see her." Martin looked back and smiled. "And to see you, of course."

Clay's throat tightened.

His father sighed. "I guess I thought by bringing Belle up here, I'd recapture some of the happiness I had with Delia." He looked past Clay's shoulder. "Maybe I was trying too hard."

One aspect of Martin's personality that had always kept Clay at arm's length was his father's capacity for melodrama—the few times he'd invested himself in whatever Martin was passionate about at the moment, he'd been left holding the bag while his father moved on to another pursuit. Clay closed his eyes against a mounting tension headache. Why couldn't life be simple?

"We're ready to go if you are," Annabelle called.

And if he didn't already have enough to worry about....

Suppressing a groan, Clay inhaled deeply for strength to turn and face what was rapidly becoming his most perplexing problem of all.

CHAPTER THIRTEEN

"SO, THE LOVEBIRDS are having second thoughts?" Michaela asked.

"Uh-huh." Annabelle sat in a chaise lounge beneath a small elm tree in her mother's back yard. "They decided to postpone the wedding and give each other a little space. Mom agreed to come back with me and stay until I'm settled into the house." She frowned up at the scant branches swaying above her. Trapped in the shadow of Martin Castleberry's towering pines, her mother's trees would never have a chance to grow. How very fitting. "We're catching a flight to Detroit the day after tomorrow."

She squirmed in the piece of wicker furniture, restless and itchy. The temperature teetered on the verge of ninety, as did the humidity level. The sky was a hodge-podge of clear patches, cottony clouds and distant charcoal-colored thunderheads. Somewhere in Atlanta it was raining, but at the moment, the real storm raged here, inside her.

"I thought that was what you wanted," Mike said, bringing her back to earth. "Why don't you sound happy?"

She laid her head back and sighed. Why, indeed? "Because Mom's been crying for the last three days." The tears wrenched her heart and reminded her of the dreadful days following her father's funeral.

Mike made a sorrowful sound. "Poor Belle. Maybe she really loves this man."

"Maybe she does," Annabelle conceded. "But that doesn't mean that Melvin—"

"—Martin—"

"—loves *her*, or will be faithful to her."

"And you're positive that he doesn't, and won't?"

She stood and rolled her neck side to side to help ease the tension in her shoulders—sleep had eluded her again last night. "Mike, the man's history with women is irrefutable."

Her friend laughed. "Always the lawyer. Can't people change?"

She frowned. "No." She thought she heard a splash from the other side of the fifteen-foot wooden privacy fence that separated her mother's backyard from the Castleberrys'. A swim would feel fabulous about right now. She wondered if it was Martin or Clay indulging in the cool water.

Or perhaps a female guest?

"People can't change?" Mike whistled. "You're being awfully defensive. What else is bothering you?"

Annabelle picked her way between the orange day-lilies toward a coin-sized hole in a fence plank left by a knot. "Nothing is bothering me. I mean, I'm sorry that my mother is upset, but she'll recover."

"Why do I have the feeling you had something to do with their little spat?"

"Clay and I—"

"Clay?" Mike cut in. "So you've been plotting with the junior Mr. Castleberry?"

She bristled at her friend's insinuating tone, and pushed away the memory of sneaking a photo of the man on their hike. "We have the same goal, that's all. And we might have given our parents a little push, but better they acknowledge their differences now rather than later."

Annabelle leaned forward and pressed her eye to the opening just in time to see Clay hoist himself up out of the pool. Her pulse surged.

"So you've been seeing a lot of him, have you?"

He stood about ten yards away, facing her, unaware he was being observed. Water rushed off his body, pulling at his dark swim trunks and emphasizing his muscular build. Not to mention his maleness. She swallowed hard.

"Annabelle?"

"Hm?"

"I asked if you were seeing a lot of the son?"

Angling for a better view, she frowned as he walked out of her vision. "I wouldn't say that."

"Is he absolutely divine?"

She straightened, suddenly sheepish, and looked around to see if anyone had caught her spying. "I honestly wouldn't know, Mike. What's going on at the office?"

"Quiet as a morgue, but at least I've had time to catch up on this cyberspace stuff. I actually logged onto the Internet to search for an apartment."

"Any luck?"

"I'm looking at two tonight. Oh, and I'll check in on Shoakie while I'm out."

"Thanks. I owe you one."

Michaela sighed dramatically. "I guess it was simply too good to be true."

"What was simply too good to be true?"

"That Mr. Right would walk up, sweep you off your feet, and take you far away from this dreary office."

"You watch too much television," she admonished her dreamy friend. "Assuming there is such a thing as Mr. Right, which I highly doubt, he's not likely to just walk up—"

The snap of a twig caused her to jerk around. Clad in jeans and a damp T-shirt, Clay stood at the edge of the back yard staring at her, one arm stretched up, leaning against a tree.

A tapping sound came across the phone. "Annabelle, are you still there?"

"Um, yes," she murmured.

Clay pointed to himself, then back down the path, indicating he'd leave if she wanted him to. She shook her head.

"What happened, Annabelle, is someone there?" her friend whispered.

"Um, yes."

"It's *him*, isn't it?" Mike squealed. "Oh, I knew it!"

"Listen, Mike," Annabelle said. "I have to run, but I'll call you back this afternoon. Thanks for handling the details surrounding the closing."

"Tell me you'll be home soon," her friend said.

"What?"

"Just tell me!"

"All right...I'll be home soon."

"And that you miss me."

"What?"

"Say it!"

"And...I miss you." She fidgeted, feeling like a fool and wondering what her friend had up her sleeve. "Goodbye." She punched a button to disconnect the call and conjured up a smile for her unexpected guest. "Hello."

He gestured toward where she stood. "What are you doing way over there?"

She realized she was standing in a bed of pine bark mulch, behind a row of thorny barberry bushes. "Um, weeding." She moved away from the fence and the telltale peephole, wincing when a briar snagged her bare knee.

His eyebrows rose. "Weeding?"

She leaned over to rip out a stray runner of Bermuda grass and held it up. "See?"

He walked closer, nodding at the phone in her other hand. "I didn't mean to interrupt your conversation."

She remembered Michaela's teasing and felt warmth travel across her cheeks. "Just checking in back home."

He studied her for a few seconds. "I hear you're leaving," he said, his tone casual. Pleasant. Nonchalant.

She nodded, stepping closer. "Yes. Mother agreed to go back with me."

His mouth quirked from side to side. "No doubt it's for the best."

He was glad to see her go—why did his words hurt her feelings so much? Wasn't she just as glad to be going? "So," she said lightly, "did you come over to offer me cash again?"

A wrinkle appeared on his forehead. "Actually, I wanted to tell you—"

"Annabelle, dear?" Belle stood in the opening of the sliding glass door, shading her eyes from the sun and looking strained.

"Yes, Mother?"

Belle stopped and touched her hair self-consciously. "Oh, Clay. I didn't realize you were here."

"Mrs. Coakley," he said with a respectful nod.

Her mother looked back and forth between them in a way that alarmed Annabelle. "Mom, did you need something?"

Belle nodded. "I was going to make a cup of tea and noticed I'm down to one bag. I don't feel like getting out, dear, with so much packing yet to do. Would you make a run to the supermarket for a few things?"

She opened her mouth to say yes, if the car would start, but Clay spoke up. "Mrs. Coakley, I was on my way out to run some errands myself—I'd be glad to take Annabelle." He looked her way for approval and she felt her head move up and down.

A distracted smile curved her mother's mouth. "Thank you, Clay." She started to go back inside, then turned. "Clay, how is your father?" Realizing it took a lot of courage for Belle to even ask, Annabelle allowed herself a moment of remorse for her part in her mother's loss.

"He's fine," Clay said without emotion. When the silence stretched around them, he added, "He said he had some business to attend to, and left early this morning."

Belle nodded, then turned and disappeared inside the house. Her mother's listlessness tugged on Annabelle's heart, and after arranging for Clay to pick her up around front, she hurried inside.

"Mom?" She walked from room to room, surprised to find her in the little study off the living room, standing inside a closet, her face buried in a checked shirt Annabelle recognized as her father's. She blinked away abrupt tears. "Mom?"

Belle swung around, her eyes shimmering. Seeming embarrassed, she smiled and stroked the threadbare shirt. "Your father wore this ratty old thing the day before his heart attack and left it hanging on the bedpost." She laughed through her tears. "He was always so bad about putting clothes in the hamper." Belle's face crumpled and she lifted her lost gaze to Annabelle. "It doesn't smell like him anymore."

Annabelle went to her mother and wrapped her arms around her, allowing her own tears to flow. "Oh, Mom, I can't imagine how much you miss Dad."

Belle clung to Annabelle and her shoulders shook. Helplessness paralyzed Annabelle, and she thought her heart might break for her mother's sorrow. But then Belle sniffed and extracted herself, visibly trying to shake her mood. "Look at me, making such a fuss."

"Mom," Annabelle said, shushing her, "you're allowed to make a fuss."

Her mother pulled a silver chain from the neck of her blouse. Annabelle teared up again at the sight of her mother's wedding ring dangling from the end.

"I thought all these schoolgirl feelings meant I was in love again," Belle murmured, fingering the worn band. "But maybe I just wanted it to be so." She pressed her trembling lips together, then said, "Maybe I'm just an old fool."

Strange, but she'd always thought of her mother as being above the simple needs of most women "Oh, Mom," Annabelle whispered, stroking away her mother's tears. "You're not a fool, you're human. Everyone wants someone to love."

Belle smiled through her tears. "Even you, Annabelle?"

She blinked and struggled for words, pushing away the image of Clay's teasing smile. "I'm not immune. I want th-that. Someday."

Belle tilted her head and her eyes softened. "I was beginning to worry that job of yours had hardened your heart."

Had it? Annabelle wondered. Had her job hardened her heart to the possibility of a love for all time? "I'm just realistic about the odds of maintaining a long-term relationship."

"You're right," Belle said, nodding. She blew her nose, then sniffed. "Martin doesn't really love me, or he'd never have given up on us so easily. I think he sees my going to Michigan as his way out."

Annabelle agreed, but remained silent. She did, however, wish she could assume some of her mother's hurt, which was palpable.

But her mother's expression suddenly changed, every feature lifting with her smile. "But I'm so lucky to have you," she said, framing Annabelle's face with her hands. "This time together will give us a chance to catch up on what's really important, and your father would like that."

Anna, promise me you'll look after your mother if something happens to me.

"Yes," Annabelle said, enormously relieved that her mother seemed on her way to healing.

"Now," Belle said, wiping her cheeks. "I'll finish packing. When you get back from the grocery, let's go through the flower bulbs I have in the garage and pick out enough to get a perennial garden started around your new house." She smiled. "Clay must be wondering where you are." She fingered a strand of hair back behind Annabelle's ear. "At least the two of you seem to have become friends."

Her heart beat a wild tattoo. "We're hardly friends, Mother."

Belle patted her hand. "Friendly, then. I'm glad my and Martin's differences haven't come between the two of you."

"Mom—"

Belle turned to rehang her father's shirt among the winter garments in the closet, then closed the door and presented a placid face to Annabelle. "We're also out of milk, dear, but a quart will do since we're leaving so soon."

And just like that, gone was Belle the woman, and back was Belle the mother.

"Of course," Annabelle said, retreating from the room. "I won't be long."

She walked through the house, confused by the emotions pulling at her heart—remorse, relief...and something unidentifiable.

Pulling apart the curtain at the living room window, she was surprised to see an oversized black pickup sitting at the end of the driveway, with Clay at the wheel. She smiled—the man was full of surprises. And in that instant, she ruefully identified the other sentiment plucking at her.

Anticipation.

Clay didn't mind waiting, because he dreaded admitting he'd been wrong about her. Henry hadn't yet delivered his report on Annabelle Coakley, but he'd come to believe he'd misjudged the young beauty—maybe she did simply have her mother's best interests at heart. She seemed eager enough to spirit Belle away to Michigan to get her out of his father's grasp.

But he frowned when he recalled the phone conversation he'd interrupted earlier. Was this Mike fellow part of the reason Annabelle was so anxious to return to Detroit?

Clay massaged the bridge of his nose because he suspected another cause for the rock of dread lodged in his chest. He was beginning to have these strange feelings—

"Sorry for the wait!"

He jerked his head around at her voice coming through the lowered passenger window. She opened the door and he leaned over to give her a hand up, gentling his grip to accommodate her slim fingers.

"Thanks," she said, breathless as she fell into the seat and closed the door with a bang. He didn't realize he was still holding her hand until she stared down at their twined fingers. With a fair amount of embarrassment, he released her. She planted her purse on the seat between them, then looked around the quad-cab pickup. "This is some truck."

Her rich-colored hair was bound up, giving him an unobstructed view of her profile—wondrously sculpted nose and chin, curving brow, jutting cheekbones. She wore denim shorts and a sleeveless green T-shirt with a yellow sunflower on the front. No makeup that he could tell, because her freckles stood out. The woman radiated health, and he was struck by his desire to put his hands around her, not to arouse himself, but simply to keep her close until he could sort through the disconcerting feelings she evoked.

Dismayed at his train of thought, he nonetheless managed a smile in her direction. "I'm not sure whether that was a compliment or an insult."

Annabelle lifted her shoulder in a half-shrug, distracted by the digital compass on the overhead console. His frustration rose a notch because he was trying to engage a serious conversation and she seemed oblivious.

"Why do you have a truck?" she pressed, looking and sounding impossibly young for a divorce attorney.

"The truck comes in handy for hauling equipment to the piece of property I own north of here." He put the vehicle in gear. "I need to run out there and drop off some papers to a surveyor—do you mind riding along?"

Her white teeth appeared on her bottom lip. "Is it far?"

Irritation jabbed him—she had more interesting things to do, like pack for her trip home to Mike. "About a twenty-minute drive, but I'll take you to the grocery and back to your mother's if you don't have time."

She pursed her pink mouth and shook her head. "That's fine. I just don't want to leave her alone for too long. Thanks for the ride, by the way. Mom's car is on its last leg."

A finger of worry nudged him when he remembered Henry's report of the women test-driving luxury sedans—was she hinting now for a new car? Was she regretting she hadn't taken the money he'd first offered her?

"How is your mother?" he asked as he pulled out of the neighborhood.

"She'll be fine," Annabelle said in a soothing tone. "She as well as admitted she was marrying Martin out of sheer loneliness. I'm sure this little romance between them has run its course. How about your father?"

"The same—a little depressed, but he seems resigned to Belle leaving." He shifted in his seat, rankled by the sensation that something worthwhile was slipping through *his* fingers. "Dad said he might even go back to Paris with me."

"I suppose you'll be returning soon then."

He nodded, suddenly realizing he'd forgotten to call the airline this morning. Too many distractions. "As soon as possible, but while I'm here, I thought I'd take care of some things at the farm."

"The farm?" Her dark eyebrows shot up.

He smiled. "It's not a farm, really, just a place where I go to clear my head." *Which is what I need right now.*

She nodded and made a thoughtful noise. "The university law library."

He glanced over. "Pardon me?"

"The university law library—it's where I go to clear my head."

Amazingly, it wasn't difficult to imagine her in a black suit and heels, with leopard-print lingerie underneath. More and more, the layers of Annabelle Coakley were being revealed to him—although not as literally as he'd envisioned in the deep of night. "Is your work schedule hectic?"

She laughed, a hearty, ruffled sound. "I handle about a hundred divorce cases a month."

He shook his head. "Sounds depressing—why do you do it?"

She stared out the window for a long time, then said, "You know, I'm starving."

He blinked at the subject change and slowed the vehicle involuntarily. "We can stop to get a bite to eat."

"A drive-through is fine," she said. "Will there be somewhere to sit once we get to your place?"

Clay looked at her lithe body, her touch-me skin, her glittering gold eyes, and had the incomprehensible urge to push the pedal to the floor and to keep driving until reality was far behind them. The compulsion to… *experience* this woman, to find out more about her was overwhelming. They were running out of time.

"Clay?"

He blinked. "Hm?"

"I asked if there would be somewhere to sit once we get there."

His body warmed, and his stomach clenched with a mixture of dread and anticipation at being alone with Annabelle. A crazy, dangerous situation, his instincts warned. He should simply take her to the grocery, stop for a to-go meal, and take her back home. And he'd never gone against his instincts.

"Clay?"

"I think we'll be able to find a spot of shade."

CHAPTER FOURTEEN

ANNABELLE MADE ONE full revolution, then turned back to Clay. "How did you find this place?"

His smile was boyishly proud as he set a bag of food on the trunk of a huge downed tree overgrown with spongy moss. "I ran across it last year while following bad directions to a golf course." He threw a jean-clad leg over the log and opened the white bag. "Needless to say, I missed my tee time."

"It's heaven," she breathed, feeling truly good for the first time since leaving Detroit. A tiny creek she could cross in one good leap hooked around a sand bank a few feet in front of them. Far, far above, boughs of top-heavy pine trees rubbed together, conversing. "How much of this land is yours?"

"Twenty-five acres, give or take."

She inhaled deeply, reveling in the eucalyptus-scented air, then walked back to straddle the log, opposite Clay. Under the low canopy of dogwood trees, she felt childlike with her legs dangling on either side of the monstrous tree, felled many years ago. She met his gaze and that strange sense of connectivity bolted through her again.

It was because they had reached their mutual goal to stop the wedding, she reasoned. Still, the intimacy of the secluded space spooked her, and she regretted suggesting that they bring lunch. The lines of his jaw, the arch of his nose, and the curve of his upper lip were becoming alarmingly familiar to her. He hadn't slept well last night, and the fact that she could tell bothered her as much as knowing he, too, had been lying awake.

Breaking eye contact to unwrap her hamburger, she strove to keep her tone light. "Based on the roll of papers you gave that man, you must be planning to build soon."

He unwrapped his sandwich and frowned. "Did you get the one with no tomatoes?"

She checked. "Uh-huh."

They traded sandwiches, and she was struck by the ease of the moment. "Are you?" she prompted after a bite. "Planning to build, I mean?"

He shrugged, chewing. "Someday. The guy I brought the papers to works for the forestry department—he's helping me put together a plan to replace some of these downed trees with a bamboo grove so I can grow some of my own materials to use when I build."

She shifted on the log—ensuring a permanent moss stain on her shorts, no doubt. Clay the naturalist didn't mesh with the picture of Clay the jet-setting workaholic she'd created in her head. "I was under the impression you don't spend a lot of time in Atlanta."

"It depends," he said, not looking up.

"On what?"

The hollows of his cheeks appeared and disappeared as he chewed slowly. "On the weather...on my bank account." He glanced up. "And on Dad."

Feigning fascination for a curly French fry, she cast about for words to form the question nagging at her. "And do you have no other ties to Atlanta?"

"I don't like strings," he said, his voice brusque as he wiped his mouth with a paper napkin.

She swallowed a too-large bite. "Then I'm sure you'll be glad when I'm gone."

His eyebrows rose a fraction of an inch.

Annabelle hurried to amend her words. "I mean when I take my mother back to Detroit."

Clay studied her for so long she flushed, wondering if her sudden, crazy physical desire for him was so evident that he was about to laugh in her face. *Another Castleberry conquest.*

Instead, he finished his sandwich, balled up the foil wrapper and dropped it in the bag, then leaned forward. "We were interrupted this morning when I was trying tell you…."

She was riveted, lulled by the sudden gentleness in his voice. *That you wished we'd met under different circumstances? That you're looking for a good attorney to help you close business in Paris?* "Tell me what?"

He inhaled, expanding his chest. "That I appreciate your help this past week." He laughed, lifting his hands in the air. "If I'd only known, I could have stayed in Paris."

Her stomach flipped. She was thinking romantic thoughts and he was thinking it wouldn't have mattered if they'd never met. "If you'd only known?"

Clay nodded. "If I'd only known that you were the perfect person to convince our folks that getting married was irresponsible."

Perhaps he had a lover in Paris. "I'm the perfect person?"

"Of course." He gestured toward her magnanimously. "You know better than anyone how disastrous marriage can be."

He spoke the truth—she'd said the same thing many times. So why did his words chafe her? Her appetite gone, she rewrapped her half-eaten sandwich and dropped it inside the bag. "Well, everybody's good at something," she said with a glib smile, drawing on the straw in her soft drink.

His inky hair, having dried a bit haphazardly from his morning swim, fell over his forehead thick and shiny. His chest and shoulder muscles occupied every inch of his cotton T-shirt, and she noticed a faint scar on his left forearm beneath the dusting of dark springy hair. His big hands rested on his thighs—at least the mystery of the calluses was solved—and she acknowledged with a feminine rush that she'd never met a more physically appealing man. Was this disjointed, prickly feeling what her mother felt when she looked at his father?

"So—" He fanned his hands and smiled. "Thanks."

He was thanking her for spreading her cynicism regarding marriage? She ran out of soda, eliciting a loud, sucking noise from her straw. "Don't mention it."

He laughed suddenly. "I was thinking it's a shame we don't live in the same city."

Her heart jerked crazily. "Why?"

"Maybe our paths would cross once in a while."

Was he hinting that he'd like to see her romantically? Annabelle attempted a small laugh. "I doubt we'd be moving in the same circles."

He gave her a dubious look. "What kinds of circles do you think I move in?"

She shrugged. "You know—gilded ones."

Clay scoffed lightly. "Only when duty dictates. I prefer more interesting company...like yours."

Suddenly, the trees seemed to be closing in on her, and the noises from the creek and insects underfoot grew to a roar in her ears. Her heart raced, and for a moment she thought she might be having a panic attack. "I need to go," she blurted, and struggled to her feet.

"Sure." He stood, easily spanning the tree trunk, and reached toward her. "Are you all right?"

She nodded, but accepted his assistance until she had both feet on the ground. The sooner they left, the sooner she could return to her mother's, and the sooner she could pack to get away from Atlanta, and the sooner she could put this blunder of the senses behind her.

"You have a leaf in your hair," he said with a crooked smile, and lifted his hand to retrieve it.

A feeling of dread washed over her because she knew he was going to kiss her again, and she knew she was going to let him. *Our last*, she justified as he lowered his lips to hers. *And best*, she instantly realized as her senses came alive. After a second's hesitation, she sighed into his mouth, leaning into him, curling her fingers around his biceps.

His embrace was so fierce, he practically lifted her off her feet. He slid his hands down her back and slipped them under the hem of her shirt to clasp her waist. She sucked his breath into her mouth as his thumbs caressed the bare skin beneath her ribs, mere inches from her peaking breasts. He transferred kisses along the line of her jaw to her earlobe, then to her neck, where he nipped at her pulse. Annabelle arched against his hard body, thrilling at his bigness, his maleness. He molded her against him, matching curve to hollow.

His breath came out in warm blasts, carrying whispers of her name, and promised pleasure, sending shivers over exposed skin.

She tried to think, really she did. A vague sense of apprehension hovered just out of reach—she shouldn't be kissing Clay, shouldn't be feeling this way, but she couldn't remember why.

One minute she was standing with her body wedged against his, and the next he had lowered her to the warm dry grass and she lay willing and wanton underneath him. Their lips and hands grew more demanding—he pushed up her shirt, she pulled his from the waistband of his jeans, he lowered his mouth to lave a peaked breast through the filmy leopard-print bra, she slid her hands over corded muscle to the small of his back. He used his teeth to pull aside the bra, she reached down to loosen his belt. Her mind and body reeled from unadulterated pleasure…this man drove her wild…made her impatient to have him.

Mounting frustration gave way to alarms sounding in her ears, rapid and staccato. Clay moaned and dragged his lips away, and she slowly realized the noise was a horn beeping from the direction they'd come.

Clay did not look happy, and she shrank from his gaze as she fell back to earth. He exhaled noisily and pushed to his feet. Hot shame flooded her as she yanked her clothes into place. She and Clay had conspired to break up their parents, and here they were rolling around like a couple of teenagers who couldn't control their urges.

"I'm sorry. I told the guy to honk if he needed something," Clay said, reaching down to help her stand.

"Go ahead," she managed, extracting her hands to wrap her arms around her middle. "I'll pick up our trash and be right there."

He studied her face for a few seconds, then nodded curtly and strode away from her, pushing past bushes and tramping through hillocks of red clay they had carefully avoided on the way down.

She started to tremble, and the lump at the back of her throat refused to subside. With much effort, she fought tears of dismay as she watched him walk away. Was this what her mother felt when she looked at Martin? Could she possibly be falling in love with Clay Castleberry? The idea seemed too incredible for her mind to embrace; indeed, a pain needled her temple. No matter, she reminded herself—this time tomorrow he'd be on his way back to Paris, and she'd be on her way back to Detroit.

Her laugh was humorless. Paris, Detroit. Fitting destinations to illustrate their differences. Glamorous versus glamour-less. She indulged in one full minute of self-pity before turning away from the sight of Clay's retreating back.

Annabelle stood in line at the supermarket tapping her foot, her restlessness fueled by the thought of Clay waiting for her in the parking lot. They'd barely spoken since leaving the secluded site. The lady in front of her in the express checkout lane had three times as many items as the limit on the sign. Oh, and great—the lane violator also wanted to write a check.

Tamping down impatience, she glanced around at the other lines, which were strung back as far as she could see. Since she'd left Atlanta, the population in the northern counties had exploded—where had all these people moved from?

Probably Michigan, she decided, whose brutal winters could certainly make one yearn for warm, sunny climates.

Looking for something to pass the time, she scanned the tabloids that lined the shelves at eye-level. The U.S. government was trying to keep the gold strike on Mars top secret. A woman in Memphis was channeling new lyrics from Elvis and the afterworld. And—

Her eyes bulged at the subtitle *Casanova Castleberry Strikes Again!* in bold red letters, story on page three. She yanked the newspaper from the stand, dropping a roll of slice and bake cookie dough in the process.

She scanned the page and zoomed in on the picture of Belle and Martin, leaning against the picnic table where they'd stopped to eat three days ago. They were locked in a torrid kiss. The copy beneath read: Is this mystery woman caught cuddling with legendary film actor Martin 'Casanova' Castleberry at an Atlanta retreat destined to be Mrs. Castleberry number six? According to diners at an Atlanta restaurant, Castleberry announced his engagement at the establishment. In the picture below, the couple was caught cavorting in the forest with Martin's son, Atlanta businessman Clayton Castleberry, and another unidentified woman. Like father, like son?

Annabelle gasped in outrage. *Cavorting?* Fury bolted through her, and she snatched every copy of the paper in the rack.

Clay played with the radio knob, trying to find something other than a sappy love song, but it appeared that the Atlanta airwaves were conspiring against him, delivering every 'can't live without her' tune ever written. Irritated, he flipped off the music, and opened the door. Never claustrophobic before, small spaces suddenly seemed to squeeze the air out of his lungs. He banged the door closed behind him and leaned against the warm metal of the truck, his eyes drawn to the exit of the grocery store, hungering for the first glimpse of her…dammit. The June sun bore down on him, relentlessly burning a sobering truth into his brain.

He had feelings for Annabelle. Strong, troubling feelings. Feelings that ran deeper than his desire for her, a longing which had already taken on a life of its own. He couldn't explain why or how this slip of a woman had managed to prick the armor he had carefully constructed around his heart, but she had. In fact, he hadn't even realized how closely he'd guarded his emotions until he met Annabelle. He'd dated many women in his life, but he'd never been distracted to the point of losing his appetite or focus, especially not by a woman with whom he'd shared little more than a few stolen kisses. But crazily, he thought of her nonstop, wanted to look at her, to spend time with her, to touch her, even if only to hold her hand. Could this distracted, out-of-body sensation possibly be love?

Had he fallen in love with this woman?

The phone in his pocket rang, offering a respite from his unsettling thoughts. He pulled it out to see Henry's name on the screen, then connected the call. "What's up, Henry?"

"Got some news on the younger Coakley woman."

Clay wiped a film of perspiration from his forehead. Whatever the man had discovered, he didn't need to know now, Clay told himself. Annabelle and her mother were going back to Detroit. The wedding plans were postponed indefinitely, and his impatient father would undoubtedly find another diversion before Belle returned. Annabelle had said she had no designs on his father's money, that she wanted to stop the wedding as much as he, and he believed her...didn't he?

"Clay, are you there?"

"I'm here," he said tightly, still staring at the exit for any sign of Annabelle.

"Well, do you want the information or not?"

Clay tried to read into the private investigator's tone. He must have uncovered some piece of incriminating information, else he would have simply said that all was clear, wouldn't he? And before he threw his heart after the woman, didn't he owe it to himself to find out if she was harboring secrets?

"Clay, man, are you there?"

"Yeah, I'm here," he snapped. "What did you find?"

"Lots of harmless stuff."

He exhaled in relief.

"Except for a couple of things," Henry continued, causing Clay's pulse to pick up again. "She inherited ten thousand dollars two years ago when her father passed away, but it isn't apparent where the money went—probably school. I looked into the information you gave me about her buying a house, and was able to get a copy of the form where she listed the source of her thirty thousand dollar down payment."

Clay's heart pounded. "Go on."

"She listed a guy by the name of Michael Horsh. I did some checking, and the man is seventy-four, divorced twice, bankrupted a couple of times, but seems to be making a go of the coffee shop he owns now."

His throat threatened to close. *Mike.* "Are they romantically involved?"

Henry grunted. "Hard to say. The Coakley woman did handle his last divorce, and they live on the same block. And according to a clerk at the coffee shop, she's a regular there. With more time, I might be able to determine a definite link between them. But according to the two marriage license applications on file, Horsh appears to prefer younger women."

"Or maybe they prefer him," Clay muttered.

"Yep."

His mind spun, assimilating the information. An older man who preferred younger women, was divorced twice and bankrupted twice, was a client of Annabelle's and had given her thirty thousand dollars for a down payment on her house. A blind man could see she was bilking this Horsh fellow.

Which probably meant she and her mother were planning to swindle his father as well. Was the postponement of the wedding a ploy to...what? To heighten his father's determination? To manipulate Martin's feelings to the point that he would forget the notion of a prenuptial agreement?

Clay swallowed. To dupe *his* heart as well?

His thoughts were interrupted by the appearance of Annabelle, her hair blowing back from her face as a blast of summer air greeted her, her eyes darting to find him. Despite the distasteful news of her work in progress in Detroit, he couldn't stop the quickening in his stomach at the sight of her. Everything in him cried out that his suspicions had been wrong, that Henry was wrong even now, that this unexplainable chemistry between them was a natural phenomenon and not a result of some scheme she'd concocted.

"Clay?" Henry said.

He snapped out of his musings, but remained riveted to Annabelle. "Anything else?" he asked abruptly.

"I'll keep digging if you want to know more."

"That's enough," Clay managed to say. "Send me a bill."

He disconnected the call and watched her glide closer to him. Loose limbed and graceful, she moved like a dancer...like a lover. Clay set his jaw.

Keep digging? He already knew so much more than he wanted to.

CHAPTER FIFTEEN

AS MUCH AS SHE wanted to shake the tabloid photo in Clay's face, she hesitated because some part of her wanted to maintain the whisper of magic they'd shared just moments ago at his farm. Illogical? Absolutely. The lawyer in her recognized the lunacy of her emotions, but she couldn't stop her fantasies, not when Clay stood next to his truck, arms crossed, looking too good for *her* good. She squinted.

Except for that frown on his face. The man was nothing if not moody.

Wordlessly, he took the grocery bag from her and walked around to help her climb inside. His hands lingered around her waist a fraction of a second longer than necessary, but overriding the desire in his eyes and in his touch, was something she couldn't put her finger on. Tension? Anger?

She studied the set of his shoulders as he walked around the front of the truck. Did he regret their lapse so much? Did he share her guilt for indulging in their attraction at the same time they were trying to drive their parents apart? She wet her lips, remembering too well the feel of his mouth claiming hers. The feel of his hands and mouth touching private places.

He deposited the bag on the seat between them, then shut the door with a bit too much force. Annabelle squirmed. He started the engine, then nodded to one of the newspapers peeking out of the bag. "I never took you for a follower of the tabloids."

Still puzzled by his attitude, she pursed her mouth. "There's a photo inside of our parents, kissing."

He frowned. "Where?"

"On the mouth!"

"I mean where was the picture taken?"

"Oh. When we were hiking the other day. I didn't see a photographer, did you?"

He glanced her way before accelerating and pulling onto the road. "The only person I remember seeing taking pictures was you."

Annabelle gasped. "Why on earth would I take a picture and turn it over to a rag like that?"

He lifted one dark eyebrow. "To perpetuate the myth that you're against this marriage."

"What?" She put a hand to her temple. "Did I miss something?"

"Yes," he said calmly, his gaze sliding to her before returning to the road. "I just received a phone call."

Confusion clogged her brain. "From whom?"

"From someone who knows about your dealings with Michael Horsh," he said, his voice terse.

Alarms sounded in her ears and heat suffused her cheeks. "Who? And what does my friendship with Michael Horsh have to do with anything?"

Anger radiated from him to fill the cab of the truck. "The fact that you wangled thirty thousand dollars from an old man in order to buy a house seems rather relevant to this situation."

Incredulity shot through her. "*What?*"

He held up his hand. "Don't pretend, counselor. You handled the man's second divorce, and he's financially strapped, yet managed to cough up the money you needed. And I assume he's the same 'Mike' you're supposed to be engaged to."

Struck speechless, Annabelle could only shake her head. How could he know these things about her, and about her friend Michael? Suddenly the appalling answer came to her. "You hired someone to investigate my personal life?"

"I had to protect my father."

An invisible hand squeezed her heart, drilling disappointment deep into her body. It was as if a curtain had descended between them. What a fool she'd been. Clay didn't care about her, he only cared about preserving the dysfunctional integrity of the Castleberry family. Why offer him an explanation when he was determined to think the worst of her? The knowledge cut to the quick, but at least she knew to a certainty where she stood.

She felt light-headed, but she refused to yield to tears. Annabelle turned her head away from him to look out the window. Caring for someone led to certain anguish. Why hadn't she listened to herself? And to Clay. After all, the man had made his opinion of long-term relationships abundantly clear. *I don't believe in happy endings.*

So why should it bother her that he didn't trust her? That he thought the worst of her? It wasn't as if they'd been headed for some kind of happily ever after. She'd been right to come to Atlanta to rescue her mother, and the sooner she and Belle were out of the vicinity of the Castleberry men, the better.

"You don't have anything to say?" he prodded, his voice tight.

Humiliation and anger flamed in her chest, and Annabelle looked back to his arrogant profile. "Yes. My first impression of you was correct. You are despicable." She blinked rapidly—she would *not* let herself cry.

He chortled without humor. "You're just cross because you got caught, Ms. Coakley." His voice was low and patronizing.

Those tears were getting harder and harder to bank. She bit down on her tongue.

"Aren't you?" he goaded.

And to think she had actually begun to believe that they shared some kind of rare emotional and physical connection. "Believe what you want to believe," she said thickly.

His jaw tensed, relaxed, then tensed again. "Don't pretend you didn't know that my father recently came into a large sum of money."

She tried to swallow past the lump in her throat. "I knew. But if money inspired me, don't you think I would have taken your bribe?" It was a monumental effort to keep her voice steady. At least they were almost home.

"Not if you thought there was more to gain by going through with the marriage." He slowed and turned into her mother's neighborhood.

"If that was the case," she said, struggling to maintain her calm, "why would I have started the argument that led to them calling off the wedding?"

"Maybe you're trying to wear me and my father down. So we'll forget the idea of a prenup."

She squinted. "*You* and your father?"

He slowed to pull onto her mother's street. "I have to give you credit for this tag-team effort," he said, his voice laced with sarcasm. "The hot and cold routine, the flirting."

"Flirting?" She moved closer to the door, as far away from him as possible. She just wanted to get away from him. Now.

He tapped his thumb on the steering wheel. "You almost had me thinking you were on the up and up, that you really weren't trying to put the squeeze on my father."

Her hurt was forgotten as white-hot anger fueled her tongue. "How dare you?" Her voice shook, and she felt dangerously close to breaking down. "There's nothing you or your father have that would remotely interest me or my mother."

He braked, poked his tongue in his cheek, and gestured toward her mother's house. "Not even a white Jaguar convertible with red leather interior?"

She followed his line of vision, then opened the door and leapt to the ground. "Mother?"

Belle and Martin sat in the sparkling convertible in her driveway, holding up flutes of champagne. A huge gold bow adorned the hood. Her mother looked up and squealed when she saw them. Waving, she yelled, "Look what Martin bought me for me, dear! Isn't it divine?"

Only disappointment topped her disbelief. The used green sedan she was having delivered for Belle would pale miserably in comparison. Worse, she could feel Clay's gloating presence even though he stood on the other side of the truck. Martin's lavish gift would only clinch Clay's suspicions. But the crowning regret was the realization that the joy on Belle's face at the reconciliation was undeniable. The woman was truly, madly, and irrevocably in love.

For a nanosecond, Annabelle was envious.

"Mother," she said, walking on rubbery legs. "What's going on?"

"The wedding is back on!" Belle beamed. "Tomorrow morning at the chapel, just the four of us!"

* * *

Clay surveyed the scene and closed his eyes to count to ten. It was just as he feared, and his father was playing right into the hands of the Coakley women. His anger was stoked by the knowledge of how close he himself came to believing...to hoping...*dammit.* "Dad," he said, striding toward the couple. "We need to talk."

"Not now, son," Martin said, dismissing him with a wave.

"Yes, now," he said forcefully.

"Clay, you're being rude," Martin admonished.

"And you're being duped," he said, gesturing to the women. "Henry has been looking into their backgrounds, and you need to know what he found."

Belle looked at his father. "Martin, what's this all about?"

Martin's face had turned a deep crimson. "Clay—"

"Just hear me out," Clay said, holding up his hand. Suddenly he couldn't bear to look at the deceitful young woman who had so effortlessly slipped under his guard. "Annabelle recently received thirty thousand dollars from her seventy-year-old fiancé in Detroit, a man named Michael Horsh."

"What?" Belle gasped. "Annabelle, what is he talking about?"

She remained silent for so long, Clay finally turned to look at her. And was not gratified by what he saw. Her arms were wrapped around her middle, and her expression was weary.

"Mr. Castleberry," she said, her voice devoid of emotion, "you seem to have misinterpreted the information your investigator dug up on me. Michael Horsh is the father of my paralegal and dear friend, Michaela. Mike, I call her."

Mike. A tiny ping of alarm sounded in his brain, similar to when he had mistaken Annabelle for his father's bride-to-be. "Why would her father give you thirty thousand dollars?" he asked smugly.

She pressed her lips together for a few seconds, then sighed. "Because I loaned him ten thousand dollars two years ago as seed money for a business he wanted to start."

"Annabelle, your inheritance?" Belle asked.

She nodded.

"But that was so risky!"

Annabelle adopted a flat smile. "A good investment, I thought, which it turned out to be. I tripled my money."

"Why didn't you ever mention it?" her mother asked.

"Because I knew you'd worry."

"But what's all this about a fiancé?" Belle asked.

Clay pursed his mouth in victory. Now he had her.

Annabelle rolled her shoulders and cleared her throat before answering. "There is no fiancé."

Belle and Martin's gaze swung back to him.

"What about her ring?" he asked, pointing to the square diamond on her finger.

"It's the ring Annabelle's father gave to me," Belle said. "I gave it to her when she arrived."

He looked at Annabelle. "But you said—"

"No, I didn't. You jumped to a conclusion and I simply allowed you to believe it."

Clay's neck grew warm. "But you were in the jeweler's trying to find out how much the ring Dad gave Belle was worth."

Their parents swung their gaze back to Annabelle.

"Yes, because I thought it was fake," she said with a sigh. "And I thought if Mom knew it was fake, that she would know she couldn't trust your father."

"Fake?" Belle asked, looking at the ring.

"It isn't," Annabelle said, walking closer to where her mother sat in the passenger seat. "In fact, the jeweler said it was of uncommonly good quality." She looked at Martin, then said, "I apologize, sir. I misjudged you." Then she looked at Clay, whose gut was clenched with dread. "Although it appears I did not misjudge your son."

His gaze locked with her golden eyes, and in two seconds, he saw the glow of what might have been diminish, then disappear completely. He wanted to say something, but his jaw seemed cemented shut, his tongue glued to the top of his mouth. She looked away, then turned a bittersweet smile toward their parents and patted her mother's hand. "I just want you to be happy, and I can see that you are."

"Yes, dear, I am."

Annabelle smiled. "Then you have my blessing."

Belle's eyes were suddenly moist. "Thank you, Annabelle."

"I'll cancel your ticket to Detroit."

"Can't you stay for just a few more days?"

"I need to get back to my office after the ceremony. Mike—I mean Michaela—will be expecting me."

Clay's stomach churned, but a movement on the street caught his attention. A late-model green luxury sedan had pulled behind the driveway, a newer car with a metal dealership sign on the door pulled in behind it.

A man alighted from the green sedan. "Is this the Coakley place?"

"Yes," Belle said, her expression puzzled.

"Got a delivery here for Belle Coakley."

Belle looked at Annabelle. "That's the car we test drove at the lot."

She nodded, her expression wry. "I bought it for you, Mom. I didn't know—" She gestured toward the Jaguar. "That is, it's nothing compared to Martin's gift."

Clay closed his eyes. That explained why the women were test-driving luxury cars. Henry had failed to tell him they were used models, probably modestly priced. Or maybe Henry had told him, and he simply hadn't heard.

"Nonsense, I love it," Belle said, handing her glass to his father and emerging from the convertible.

"Don't worry, Mom. The dealership will refund the money. Besides, I should have asked you."

Belle bit on her lower lip, then stroked Annabelle's face. "It was a wonderful gesture, dear, but I'm a grown woman and I can take care of myself."

Annabelle's smile was apologetic. "I'll tell the man we changed our minds," she said, then walked to the curb.

Clay's chest tightened when he saw her smile up at the salesman, and the way the man responded to her. He leaned toward her, nodding his understanding. And his handshake lingered for far too long. Clay took one step in their direction before pulling himself back with a stern reprimand. What was he doing?

"All taken care of," Annabelle said to her mother as she walked back up the driveway. She gave Belle a quick kiss. "And now I'd better take care of the tickets."

She turned to go inside, and at last Clay found his voice. "Annabelle, wait."

She stopped, one foot on the bottom step, but she didn't turn back.

Clay walked to her, his heart pounding. "Why—" He cleared his gravelly throat and touched her arm. Her skin felt soft, but cold. "Why did you let me believe you were engaged?"

Her eyes were mocking, and she seemed to look past his shoulder. "I thought you would leave me alone if you believed I was engaged," she murmured for his ears only. She pulled away from his grasp, then climbed the steps and disappeared into her mother's house.

Her words twisted his gut, and he gripped the handrail to keep from going after her. She found him that loathsome? What did it matter anyway? Clay set his jaw, and whirled around to face two sets of accusing eyes.

Martin shook his head. "You crossed the line this time, Clay."

Frustration, anger, and guilt pummeled him, elevating his voice. "I was doing it for you, Dad." He stubbornly clung to his original argument, his pride smarting that his own father couldn't see the sacrifice he'd made to save him from yet another landmine.

"Maybe," his father said, alighting from the car and closing the door slowly. "Lord knows I've made mistakes in the company I've kept, but it's obvious to me as it should be to you how fortunate I am that Belle will have me." He gave her a fond smile, then looked back, his expression hardening. "But frankly, son, sometimes I think you meddle in my life as a diversion to your own unhappiness."

Clay's chin jerked up at his father's preposterous words. "My life is perfectly fine," he said through clenched teeth. "The fact that you're trying to turn this situation back on me is proof that you're making another mistake."

In fact, for all he knew, Annabelle and her mother could have concocted that entire little explanation in case their scheme was divulged. Desperation spiraled in his stomach. Deep down, he knew he wasn't making sense, not even to himself. But if Annabelle wasn't a conniving, hard-hearted, selfish gold-digger, then that meant she was an intelligent, warm-hearted, caring daughter. And he wasn't ready to admit that he had so woefully miscalculated her motives. And her heart. And her kisses.

His father's expression was rueful. "I'm sorry you feel that way, son. Because Belle and I would like to have your blessing too."

He straightened, anxious to distance himself from this messy, complicated affair. Let his father fend for himself—he was through.

"I'll be returning to Paris as soon as possible," he said in a clipped tone. Clay wheeled and strode toward his truck, determined to outpace the fierce doubt nipping at his heels.

CHAPTER SIXTEEN

CLAY'S THUNDEROUS MOOD followed him on the drive to his condo. Even the sight of the freshly painted white walls couldn't cheer him up. The place seemed cold and sterile, the furniture stiff and unwelcoming. He walked around the five-room luxury accommodations, watering neglected plants and opening blinds to fill dark corners with light.

Funny, but all these furnishings the decorator had carefully selected to make his place homey seemed to have achieved the opposite effect. The leather chairs, the granite-top tables, the pewter statues—he might as well be standing in a showroom. No family relics here, no antiques or sentimental what-nots. No photos, save the one of his mother in a silver picture frame on the hall table—one of his few contributions to the décor. This barren place wasn't a home, it was the quarters of a permanent guest.

Indulging a scowl, Clay sifted through his mail—none of it personal—and turned on his laptop in a futile attempt to immerse himself in work. Paging through an array of urgent e-mail messages from impatient clients, he mentally kicked himself. If only he'd stayed in Paris, he'd have closed the investor deal, maybe two. But more importantly, he would have never met Annabelle Coakley.

Annabelle Coakley, with her lioness eyes and her freckled nose and dimpled cheeks. And scorching kisses that promised pleasures he would never know. The hauntingly beautiful face that could be soft with vulnerability, or flushed with anger. An attorney who worked long hours for little pay and scant respect. A loving daughter who missed her father and seemed bent on protecting her mother. He'd mistaken her for a ditzy pushover, and in the end, she'd doled out more grief to him than he'd ever dreamed of giving her. Or rather, he'd brought the grief on himself by crossing her at every opportunity.

He'd toyed with the idea of calling Henry to check out the explanation Annabelle had given concerning her relationship to the older man in Detroit and the money that had exchanged hands. But now, removed from the moment, he knew in his gut she was telling the truth. Something in her eyes when she'd said, "I thought you would leave me alone if you believed I was engaged," had cut him deep.

Was he that much of an ogre? Clay sat back in his chair and rubbed his eyes with forefinger and thumb. Considering the way he'd greeted her, tried to bribe her to leave, kissed her roughly, he couldn't blame her. She'd come to Atlanta thinking the worst of the Castleberrys and his behavior since had only reinforced her opinion. Although his subsequent kisses had been administered with somewhat less menace, she nonetheless had maintained a determined distance from him. She might have endured his kisses—maybe even enjoyed them—but she didn't trust him. Didn't respect him.

Didn't even *like* him, much less love him.

He grimaced at the manifestation of the word that had been hovering on his mind for hours. These absurd feelings… guilt? Sure. Remorse? Maybe. But love?

Frankly, son, sometimes I think you meddle in my life as a diversion to your own unhappiness. What utter nonsense. He was perfectly happy. Perfectly. Clay pushed away from his desk and walked to the kitchen for a cold bottle of beer. Afterward, something drove him to the hallway where his mother's image waited, smiling up at him like the movie star she was.

What did he know about love except the distant memories of his mother? He picked up her photo and studied her eyes, willing her to impart a bit of wisdom into his head and heart.

"You would like her, Mother. She's smart, pretty, and completely unimpressed with me, just like you were with Dad."

She smiled, and he could imagine her nodding her approval.

"How do I know if I love her?" he murmured.

She smiled, and suddenly he remembered his mother's words as she tucked him in bed one night. She'd been wrapped in a silvery robe, her hair cascading around her gentle face.

"I love you, Clay."

Her words had filled him with joy, and he'd wanted to prolong her visit to the edge of his bed. "Why do you love me, Mommy?"

"Because," she'd said, leaning forward to rub her nose against his, "your heart calls out to mine."

Clay closed his eyes and bit down on his lip. Did Annabelle's heart call out to his? He let out a bitter laugh. After the way he'd treated her, the only thing her heart was likely to call out to him was obscenities. He had nothing with which to compare these prickly, plaguing feelings, but he knew therein lay a generous amount of guilt and a staggering dose of desire.

He lifted the beer bottle to his mouth. But love?

No. Not him. Besides, he'd just jeopardized a sizable deal to come back and convince his father that marriage was a farce. How big of an idiot would he have to be to fall in love while trying to stop his father's wedding?

Pretty damn big. And he hadn't built his career and reputation by conducting himself like an idiot. He swallowed a mouthful of the bittersweet liquid. No, he most certainly wasn't in love.

"I'm not in love," he said aloud in affirmation.

His mother smiled.

"I'm not," he said with more vehemence. "Just to prove it, I'm calling the airline right now. By the time the so-called wedding takes place, I'll be in Paris, far away from Annabelle Coakley."

He couldn't be sure, but for a second he thought his mother smiled a little less.

"So the wedding is back on?" Michaela asked.

"Yes, tomorrow."

"You sound resigned."

"I am," Annabelle said with a sigh. "And Mom will be fine—I believe I underestimated her judgment." It was her own judgment, it seemed, that was lacking.

"I can't believe the son turned out to be such a jackass."

"Yeah." Her heart still squeezed when she remembered the look on his face, accusing her of trying to swindle him and his father, insinuating that she'd cozied up to him so he'd lower his guard. He had no idea what those kisses and intimate moments and bits of personal revelation had cost her. Didn't she counsel women every day not to let their emotions overrule their common sense? A fine role model she'd turned out to be.

"Annabelle?"

She yanked her attention back to phone call. "Hm?"

"I said don't let him get to you. I mean, it's not like you care what he thinks of you, right?"

Annabelle bit into her lower lip. Mike had hit the nail on the head—she wasn't bothered so much by the fact that Clay had looked into her background as she was by the fact that he had so easily drawn the worst conclusion from the circumstantial evidence. Sure, she'd believed the worst of him when they'd first met, but over the past several days, her opinion of him had shifted as she'd gotten to know him. In fact, she'd fancied herself to be falling for him, had imagined an uncommon connection with him. What a joke, since his opinion of her apparently hadn't changed at all. The fact that he would have made love to her that afternoon on his property despite his low opinion of her made her stomach roll. And the fact that she might have allowed him to made her feel decidedly ill.

"Right, Annabelle?"

"Right."

"Are you okay? You sound strange."

"I'm fine. I'll call you when I get back in town."

"Okay," Mike said, sounding hesitant. "I feel bad that I was teasing you about falling for this guy. Guess I was dead wrong about him."

"Bad judgment seems to abound."

Mike paused. "Is there something you want to tell me, boss?"

So perceptive, this one. "No, nothing at all. I'll see you soon."

Annabelle disconnected the call, then on impulse, pulled up the photo she'd taken of Clay the day of the hike, leaning against a rock and looking uncharacteristically surprised. The fact that the man wasn't used to being caught off-guard had made the picture even more special, because for the briefest second, Clay Castleberry had appeared...exposed. Vulnerable. Approachable. On hindsight, however, the expression had been a trick of the light.

Brimming with sadness and anger and longing, her finger hovered over the delete button. But at the last second, she couldn't bring herself to do it—a fact that bothered her even more.

The room was bathed in late evening moonlight. An open window siphoned in the muted sounds of the sultry night—cicadas, night birds, and the occasional hum of a car. The rumble of a plane's engine sounded in the distance, and she wondered if Clay was already in the air. It would seem so, given his hasty exit. And it was for the best. Annabelle sighed, stretched out on her old bed and hugged a pillow to her chest.

She had every reason to be happy. After all, Belle was marrying a man who cared about her. When she returned to Detroit, she wouldn't have to worry about her mother being lonely or unsafe. She was convinced her mother's heart was in the right place, and although Belle's second marriage would bear little resemblance to her first, she deserved the right to have grown and changed as a woman.

After all, she thought miserably—every woman changed. She squeezed her eyes shut. Hadn't she? Hadn't she arrived in Atlanta spoiling for a fight? Unable to believe her mother could fall in love in such a short time? Now the joke was on her—she'd lost her heart in a matter of days, with a man who stopped just short of despising her. Oh, he'd stolen kisses in the heat of a charged moment, but only to prove he was capable of lording over her. A tear slipped out and curled around her cheek. How he must be gloating. Sitting in first class winging his way back to Paris, smirking over how he'd so easily manipulated her into accepting—even anticipating—his touch.

At least her mother had fallen in love with a man who mirrored her feelings. She, on the other hand, had fallen for a cold, cynical, scheming, condescending man who would never appreciate or accept her love. Clay Castleberry had made the situation crystal clear: Her love was wasted on him. Unfounded and unwanted.

So why couldn't she simply dismiss him from her normally logical mind?

A knock on her door made her sit up and rub her thumbs over her damp eyes. "Yes?"

Her mother's gentle face appeared in the doorway. "Annabelle, dear, are you feeling well?"

She conjured up a bright smile. "Just a mild headache from all the excitement, I suppose."

Belle walked over to sit on the edge of the bed next to her. "Excitement indeed. I can't remember when so much transpired in so little time."

"Are you all packed?"

"Yes, mostly shorts and cool dresses. Hawaii will be even warmer than here." Her mother's smile was balm to her scuffed heart. "Thank you, my dear."

Puzzled, Annabelle asked, "For what?"

"For giving us your blessing today. More than anything in the world, I want you to be happy for me."

"I am, Mother. I believe you and Martin will have a good life together."

Belle tilted her head. "Even without a prenuptial agreement?"

Annabelle smiled. "Even without a prenuptial agreement."

Her mother picked up Annabelle's left hand and studied the engagement ring she'd worn for thirty years. "I'm glad you've softened toward Martin, but I wish you would soften toward the idea of marriage for yourself someday."

She bit down on her tongue to stem the tears of self-pity. *I-yie-yie*, if her mother only knew. Pining for a man whose interest in her extended only to illicit groping. "Mother, I'm not as hardened to the idea as you might think," she said carefully. "I just haven't found someone as compatible as you and Martin seem to be."

Her mother cleared her throat. "As far-fetched as it may sound, Martin and I were rather hoping there would be a romantic spark between you and Clay."

Her throat convulsed.

"But after his appalling behavior today, I can see we were mistaken about the match." She patted Annabelle's hand. "Martin is extremely upset with him."

Annabelle shook her head. "I don't blame Martin for his son's actions. In fact," she said thickly, "I was just as guilty as Clay for wanting to find some reason to stop the wedding."

Belle clucked. "At least you were willing to own up to your mistakes. Clay seems bent on believing the worst, and I don't like anyone misjudging my baby."

A warm feeling of security wrapped around her shoulders, making her appreciate just how ludicrous her idea of swooping in to save her mother had been—Belle was the rock, the foundation upon which their family had rested. The irony of her father's plea for her to take care of her mother showed just how well Belle had fostered the illusion that she was dependent upon them. Even Annabelle had believed it. But now, looking into her mother's wise blue eyes, she realized she should be so lucky to one day possess her mother's strength and capacity to love.

"I adore you, Mom," she whispered.

Her mother leaned forward and touched her forehead to Annabelle's. "And I adore you." Belle pulled back and smoothed Annabelle's hair away from her face. "It means so much to me that you're staying to witness the ceremony tomorrow."

Remorse stirred in her chest. "I'm glad you still want me there after all the trouble I caused."

"Shush, of course I want you there. And so does Martin. I think it takes the sting out of Clay going back to Paris."

Annabelle averted her gaze and bit her tongue against the lump of emotion that blocked her throat.

"Don't worry, dear, you'll never have to see the man again."

Her mother had verbalized the fear that had hovered in the back of her brain since she'd last seen Clay at the foot of the steps. She pressed her lips together, and her jaws ached from clenching her teeth, but she was helpless to stop the tears that spilled over her cheeks.

Her mother's eyes flew wide, then narrowed. "Annabelle, there's more going on here than injured feelings, isn't there?"

She nodded wretchedly.

Belle leaned over and removed a tissue from a box on the nightstand, then held it out. "Tell me."

Annabelle wiped her eyes, then blew her nose and exhaled a cleansing breath. "Nothing to tell really. I misinterpreted Clay's interest."

"Interest?" Her mother pursed her mouth. "I see. You're in love with him?"

She lifted her shoulders. "I think I fell in love with the *idea* of him. Infatuated, maybe, with a man who's different than anyone I've ever known."

Belle cleared her throat delicately. "Did he...did you...?"

Annabelle's eyebrows shot up. "Oh, no. Which makes this situation even more bewildering because we've barely spent any time together. But I thought I was getting to know him. I thought...." She gave a self-deprecating laugh. "I was obviously out of my league, not to mention out of my mind."

Her mother angled her head. "I know you're hurting now, but opening your heart to someone else is nothing to be ashamed of. The fact that Clay is blind to your feelings is his loss."

"You sound suspiciously like a biased mother."

Belle smiled. "I don't think you should take Clay's behavior personally, dear. Martin said he's always had a thorny personality where women are concerned. But if it's any consolation, Martin also said that the way Clay looked at you gave him hope that he'd someday settle down."

One side of her mouth pulled back. "Apparently he was just trying to scope out my weaknesses."

Her mother reached forward to stroke Annabelle's cheek. "I'm glad to see your sense of humor returning."

In truth, she was feeling minutely better. Just confessing her lapse of judgment concerning Clay eased the tightness in her chest. She laid her head back against the headboard and stifled a yawn.

"It's lights out for you," Belle said, suddenly all mother as she stood and fussed with the covers on the bed. "I can't have my maid of honor falling asleep in the middle of the ceremony tomorrow."

She smiled up at her mother, savoring the intimacy of the moment. "Mom, why do you think I fell for Clay of all men, and why now of all times?"

Belle's eyes danced as she tucked the covers under Annabelle's chin. "That's the most mysterious thing about love—it takes hold of you whether you're ready or not."

She swallowed. "But it hurts."

"It's supposed to. Otherwise, you wouldn't notice." Belle leaned forward and kissed her. "But the sun will rise tomorrow."

"I hope it's a beautiful day for your wedding."

Belle smiled. "It will be, regardless of the weather." Then she whispered goodnight and crept to the door.

With a surge of admiration, Annabelle wondered when her mother had become so wise to the ways of the heart. "Thanks for listening, Mom."

"You're welcome. Try to get some rest."

The door closed, and Annabelle dutifully began to count sheep. She owed it to her mother not to look like a puffy-eyed, heartbroken discard on one of the happiest days of Belle's life. Annabelle sniffled. After tomorrow, however, she couldn't make any promises.

CHAPTER SEVENTEEN

INDEED, IT WAS A beautiful day, and Belle was a blushingly lovely bride dressed in pink, with white flowers in her hair.

Martin looked dashing in black, and Annabelle was reminded of the day she had watched Clay being fitted for a similar jacket. The day he had stepped in to save her from certain humiliation and possible ruin. The day she had first begun to see him in a different light. In retrospect, though, he had probably believed her to be a thief and had intervened only to keep his father's name out of the incident. She burned with shame at how grossly she'd misinterpreted nearly every move the man had made. With great effort, she forced her mind back to the moment at hand, and pasted a smile on her face as the minister called everyone to the front of the church.

She gave her mother a quick kiss and hugged Martin. He flashed her a regretful smile that said her mother had confided the extent of her feelings for his son. Poor man, his eyes kept darting to the door of the church on the hope, she knew, that Clay would somehow materialize.

But it was not to be.

Since the wedding party consisted only of the bride and groom, the minister, the organist, the photographer, and Annabelle, the wedding march was dispensed with, but Annabelle teared up anyway as soon as the music began. Her heart was full of love for her mother, sweet memories of her father, and hope that she herself would someday find someone to share her life. Who knew that her trip to Atlanta would bring such a revelation? Her tears fell unchecked as the minister began the service.

"Dearly beloved, we are gathered here on this blessed day to witness the union of Martin Castleberry and Belle Coakley. Marriage is a holy institution, not to be entered into lightly, but with reverence and with love."

Belle and Martin smiled at each other and clasped hands. With a rush of affection, Annabelle decided that her father would approve of the marriage, would be happy to know that Belle was no longer alone, no longer lonely.

"If anyone knows why this man and this woman should not be married, then let him speak now or forever hold his peace."

"Stop the wedding!"

Annabelle turned, along with everyone else, at the sound of Clay's booming voice. The organist blasted out a crash of wrong notes, then silence burst around them.

Clay stood at the back of the church, dressed for traveling in casual slacks and shirt. His face was an immobile mask. Annabelle's heart lodged in her throat, followed by quick resentment that he would mar the day for his father by creating a spectacle.

The minister peered over his spectacles. "Who are you?"

"I'm his son," Clay said, striding toward them. "And I can't in good conscience see this wedding take place—"

"Clay—" Martin began.

"Without giving my father my blessing."

Annabelle inhaled sharply in pleasant surprise.

Clay stopped in front of Martin and gave him an apologetic smile. "If you'll have it, that is."

Martin's face creased in a wide grin and he clapped Clay on the back. "You've made me a very happy man, son. I'm glad you made it."

The men embraced heartily, and over his father's shoulder, Clay's gaze met hers. Annabelle was happy for father and son, but their reconciliation didn't change the things he'd accused her of, the things he believed her to be. She glanced away, her cheeks stinging from dried tears.

As the minister proceeded with the ceremony, she tried to concentrate on the words being exchanged, but she felt Clay's silent presence just as tangibly as that first day on the train from the airport, crowding her mind and her body.

Her eyes burned, and breathing became increasingly difficult, but she scrupulously avoided making eye contact with him across the aisle.

She silently urged the minister to hurry, but the man seemed eager to compensate for the small audience by bestowing many glad tidings, words of wisdom, and prayers upon the happy couple. Finally he pronounced them man and wife. "You may kiss the bride."

Annabelle stepped back so the photographer could get a good shot, and bumped into someone. "I'm sorry," she murmured, but before she even turned around, she instinctively knew it was Clay. She steeled herself for his intense gaze, and looked up.

"It was my fault," he said, his blue eyes studying her face. "Can you ever forgive me?"

She pulled a little laugh from thin air. "It was only a little bump—no harm done."

He pressed his lips together. "I meant all of it, this entire mess was of my making. I behaved abominably, and I wouldn't blame you if you never spoke to me again."

So he wanted them to be friends, or at least friendly. For their parents' sake, no doubt, but she'd rather not have to pretend. Besides, the more time she spent around Clay, the more likely the chance he'd notice that her feelings for him ran deeper than "friendly." And she'd suffered enough humiliation at his hand.

"Then we have an understanding," she said lightly. "I won't speak to you, and you won't blame me."

He flinched. "I deserve that. But if you won't talk to me, then please listen. I'm sorry for doubting you, for doubting your motives. I'm so accustomed to everyone around me having an angle, I'd forgotten that there are still honest, caring people in the world."

She swallowed hard.

"I wanted to believe that you were capable of those things I accused you of, because I wanted to find a reason to dismiss the way I'd begun to feel about you."

Her heart jerked crazily, but she refused to allow her imagination to take flight. He only wanted for the two of them to be on civil terms. Clay picked up her hand gently and squeezed it. At his warm, powerful touch, all the misunderstandings and hateful words faded from memory. With a sinking heart, she knew she'd take whatever measure of friendship he had to offer, and would keep her feelings for him tucked away in her heart. In time, perhaps she could look upon him as a mere friend. At least they wouldn't have to be adversaries.

"You once said that in my job, I was a glorified matchmaker," he said. "That I knew when two people belonged together."

He lifted her hand to his mouth for the briefest kiss, and her eyes widened in surprise—and anticipation.

"I believe you and I belong together, Annabelle, and even if you don't feel the same, I had to come back and let you know how I feel. It's the least I owe you after the way I treated you." His chest rose with a deep inhale, then he gave her a smile so tender that moisture welled in her eyes. "Your heart calls out to mine, Annabelle. Heaven knows that I don't deserve another chance with you, but if you'll grant me one, I'd be the happiest man alive."

Emotion clogged her throat. The words that escaped her were hoarse and hesitant. "But you said you don't believe in happy endings."

He cupped her chin and searched her face. "I love you, Annabelle. Do you have any similar feelings for me?"

She swallowed hard, then nodded tearfully. "Yes."

His breath whooshed out. "Then I'm a believer." He lowered his head and she met his lips for a kiss so intense, so full of promise and passion that she forgot they were standing in a church with an audience until her mother's voice penetrated her senses.

"Annabelle!"

They parted in time for Annabelle to see something hurtling toward her. Out of pure instinct, she held out her hands...and caught her mother's bouquet.

EPILOGUE

ANNABELLE LIFTED her glass of champagne toward Belle and Martin. "Happy anniversary!"

"I'll second that," Clay said, joining in the toast to mark the one-year milestone of their parents' wedding. With his free hand, he squeezed Annabelle's shoulders.

She smiled up at the man she loved with all her heart. With a little start, she noted an ease of tension around his deep blue eyes that even she hadn't been aware of before. Realization dawned. Although Clay had wholeheartedly supported their parents' wedding and hadn't voiced any doubts since, deep down he must have harbored some measure of concern that his father would disappoint Belle and renege on his promise to her...on his promise to all of them. Unbeknownst to Annabelle, Clay must have set this date, their parents' one-year anniversary, as a benchmark in his mind, because none of Martin's marriages since his first had made it past this point. The fact that Clay had been figuratively holding his breath tugged on her heartstrings—he so wanted to believe in his father.

And now he did.

When Martin came over to hug his son, Annabelle happily released him, gratified that in the past year, father and son had developed the kind of relationship she knew Clay had always longed for.

Belle met her for a fierce hug. "I'm so glad you're here, my love."

"I wouldn't have missed this, Mom."

"We're all counting the days until your employment contract is up with the state."

"Forty-three days," Annabelle said with a laugh. She, too, was counting, and her anxiety level grew every time she X'd another day off her calendar.

Belle shot a glance toward Clay. "Clay, especially, can't wait until you're free."

Annabelle blushed. "Clay and I haven't talked about what will happen when my contract expires. I like my house. And things have been good—he flies in every other weekend or so, and we Skype when he's in Europe."

"Still, it's not the same as being together all the time."

"I know," Annabelle said, "but I'm not sure we should rock the boat." Her stomach churned at the lie...what she wasn't sure about was whether Clay had gotten over his aversion to marriage. She knew he loved her, but marriage—that was something else altogether. And she'd detected a recent change in his demeanor. He'd grown more quiet and distracted, which she'd attributed to an important deal he was trying to close that seemed to be requiring a lot of his time. But when she'd asked about it, he had been evasive about the details, citing confidentiality. And the last couple of times he'd visited, she'd caught him staring at her calendar where she was counting down the days of her contract. Was he feeling pressured?

Second guessing a happily ever after?

And truth be told, she still had her own issues with marriage and whether she was suited for it. She couldn't imagine not being with Clay the rest of her life...but every day she saw firsthand how marriage changed people.

But not Martin and Belle, thank goodness, who were even more in love now than a year ago.

"What a beautiful cake," Annabelle said, nodding to the gaily decorated layer cake on the table next to the pool where they were cooking out.

"The Nelsons sent it," Belle said. "They're the best neighbors Martin and I could ever have."

Annabelle smiled, happy the young family who had moved into the home she'd grown up in had adopted Martin and Belle as grandparents.

Especially since she knew they were both eager for grandchildren of their own.

She lifted her glass for another sip of champagne, telling herself she shouldn't be thinking about anything today except the happy occasion at hand.

"Let's get those steaks on," Martin said, moving toward the massive grill he commandeered whenever they cooked out. Clay seemed especially eager to help his dad. Annabelle tried not to feel slighted that he seemed to be avoiding her on this trip...after all, today wasn't about them and their relationship.

She set aside her apprehension and focused on enjoying the evening. Belle and Martin were planning an extended trip to Los Angeles where Martin was filming a movie of the week. Belle was atwitter with excitement at the stars they would be socializing with while they were there, and how some of the female celebrities she'd idolized were in reality so down to earth, and had asked for her recipe for Tomato Cheese Pie.

After a dinner and dessert that left them all stuffed, she and Clay said goodnight to the happy couple and climbed into Clay's pickup to head toward his Buckhead condo. Over the past year, he'd asked for her help to make the place more homey, but she still felt like a visitor there...unless she was in his arms in his king-sized bed.

She studied his handsome profile in the low lighting of the cab and gave in to the thrill that barbed through her every time she looked at him. Even after a year, he still moved her. Her body hummed in anticipation of their lovemaking later tonight—seeing each other so infrequently certainly kept the fires burning in that department. There were no questions about their physical compatibility...it was other areas of their relationship that she'd suddenly begun to question.

"It was a nice night, wasn't it?" he asked.

"So nice," she agreed. "Our parents are lucky to have found each other—they seem so simpatico in every respect."

A few months ago, he might've reached over to clasp her hand and say they, too, were simpatico. He did reach over to wrap his big hand around hers, but he remained silent.

Annabelle's heart squeezed. Then she looked out the window and squinted. "Are we heading north?"

He stared straight ahead. “I need to check on something at the property—do you mind?”

“Of course not.” But unease blipped in her stomach—was he trying to delay being alone with her in the condo? She squashed her unsettling thoughts, conceding she hadn’t seen the property in months. Since that first interrupted kiss next to the mossy log, they’d shared lots of stolen moments there in the grass... next to the creek...in the grass...in the grass.

At this late hour, though, he probably wanted to check on the irrigation system that fed the stands of bamboo that were proliferating on the land. He’d recently provided a sample of the bamboo to Zoo Atlanta for feeding the giant pandas who were finicky about their greens. Apparently, the bamboo had been a hit because zoo officials had contacted him to see how much more he could provide.

While she had been excited about the novelty of the project, she’d wondered if it had supplanted Clay’s plans for building a house there someday, if he was rethinking his future.

When they pulled onto the property and bumped along a dirt road, she was reminded how dark it could be away from the lights of the traffic and the city. The stars above them were like holes punched into an inky blue canopy. The headlights of the truck spot-lighted tall grass, rolling rises, and towering bamboo stands that had grown exponentially since the last time she’d seen them. She rolled down her window and leaned out to listen to the crickets and the grasshoppers that never slept. It was a perfect summer night—still warm from the day’s heat, but enough of a breeze to keep the humidity at bay.

“I’d almost forgotten how pretty it is,” she said, thinking how much she would miss it if...

If it turned out that she and Clay weren’t simpatico.

He slowed the truck to a stop next to a metal box the size of a small chest. He turned off the engine, but left the headlights on to guide his way to the box. After unlocking a small door on the box, he reached inside to pull a switch. A few yards away, a newly erected dusk to dawn light on a tall pole buzzed to life, illuminating the ground beneath it.

Annabelle climbed out of the truck and stared at the large area that had been staked off with yellow tape. “What’s this?”

“My house.”

Hurt stabbed her. So Clay was moving ahead with his plans, and he hadn’t even told her. She couldn’t look at him.

“Actually,” he added, his voice sounding hoarse, “it’s *our* house...hopefully.”

Her heart beat a tattoo against her breastbone as she swung her head around. “Hopefully?”

He bit into his lip and took her hand. “Annabelle, I know how you feel about getting married...and I’ve always felt that way, too.”

“Clay, I—”

“Please let me finish before I lose my nerve.”

She clamped her mouth shut. Clay, lose his nerve?

“I know this sounds old-fashioned to you, but I don’t want a long-distance relationship, and I don’t want us to just live together.” His throat convulsed. “I’d like for you to move back here when your work contract expires, but if not, I’m prepared to move to Michigan. So I thought I’d better ask before I broke ground on the foundation.”

Her mind swirled with his revelations. “Ask what?”

“Seeing our parents celebrate their anniversary today confirmed what I want for us.” He lowered to one knee and pulled a small velvet box from his pocket.

Annabelle inhaled sharply and her blood rushed in her ears.

He opened the box to reveal a sparkling diamond-studded band to perfectly complement her mother’s engagement ring. “Annabelle Coakley, will you marry me?”

She was speechless. A few minutes ago she was sure she was about to have her heart broken. And now, her heart was so big in her chest, it felt as if it might burst anyway. Any doubts she had about matrimony disintegrated when she looked into his eyes. How could she ever have thought she would be satisfied with anything less than being married to this man? She wanted to be legally bound to him...for better or for worse...for richer, for poorer...in sickness and in health...until death parted them...after many, many years in each other's arms.

Still, she couldn't resist toying with the man a bit—after all, she had a reputation to maintain.

She crossed her arms. "Marry you?"

He nodded solemnly, his expression anxious.

"Would I have to sign a prenuptial agreement?"

"No."

"Would I have to change my name?"

"No."

"And I wouldn't have to move?"

"No."

She pulled her hand over her mouth and pretended to consider her options, but the joy bubbling in her chest wouldn't allow her to maintain the sham. She laughed through her fingers and Clay's head came up.

"I'd marry you anyway, Clay Castleberry." She went into his arms. He stood and spun her around, laughing. When he set her down, he pushed the ring onto her finger, then kissed her hard.

As his warm mouth moved over hers, Annabelle's mind went back to the first time he'd kissed her and how far they'd come since that fateful day. That kiss had been born of lust, but this kiss was a promise of their life together. When they ran out of breath, they clung to each other.

"I was sure you'd say no," he murmured against her hair. "I've been so worried. And afraid you'd be suspicious because planning the house has been taking so much time."

She pulled back. "*This* is your confidential project?"

He nodded. "I've been working with the builder to get the house sited."

He grabbed her hand and pulled her toward the staked off area, then stepped over the yellow tape that delineated the outside walls. "I was thinking the front door would be there...and the kitchen would be there...and the living room would be there, with huge picture windows looking down the valley." He stopped and looked up, his face going from hopeful to contrite. "But we can make any changes you want, of course."

Annabelle laughed. "I'm sure it will be grand." She glanced around, then gave him a mischievous smile. "And where will the bedroom be?"

He grinned and pointed to a corner. "Over there." He twined their fingers and led her to a grassy spot. He held her gaze as he pulled his blue dress shirt out of his waistband and unbuttoned it. Her mouth watered as the flat planes of his stomach and broad chest were revealed. His amazing physique stirred her more now than the first time she saw him swimming in his pool, mocking her. Because now she knew the pleasure his body could deliver to hers.

He shrugged out of the shirt, then spread it over the soft grass. He reached for her and pulled her down on top of him, claiming her mouth for a tender, sweet kiss. They were practiced lovers now, intimate with each other's bodies and pressure points and noises. Yet something had changed—it felt like the first time all over again.

Their clothes were discarded with deliberate slowness, skin was caressed and pleasure centers aroused with aching care. When their bodies met, they stroked each other to a fierce release that mirrored how their love had expanded with a deepened commitment.

"I love you," Clay murmured in her ear, while their bodies recovered.

"I love you, too," Annabelle whispered, trailing her hand over his heart.

A smile curved her mouth as she marveled how much her life had changed in a mere year. She lifted up on one elbow. "What will we do if someone tries to stop *our* wedding?" she teased.

He emitted a low growl and pulled her close for another kiss. "Let them try."

- The End -

A NOTE FROM THE AUTHOR

Thank you so very much for taking the time to read my romantic comedy STOP THE WEDDING! I love to write stories like this that are uncomplicated and fun reads, good for an afternoon of entertainment. I was happy to set this book in my hometown of Atlanta to drop in some authentic local details, including the encroachment of huge home developments on older, established neighborhoods. In this book, I used the juxtaposition of the two homes to further illustrate the differences in the Coakley/Castleberry households! I also enjoyed writing the relationship between mother and daughter. In the beginning, Annabelle is so sure her mother doesn't know how to handle herself as a single woman, she cartwheels into Atlanta thinking she's going to teach her a thing or two about men and relationships. But I love Belle's quiet wisdom and patience as she schools her adult daughter in the ways of the heart. I've always envisioned STOP THE WEDDING! as a movie—I could think of some great actors to play Martin and Belle and Clay and Annabelle, and I think the physical comedy would really come alive on a screen in a way it can't always on paper. Who knows—maybe I'll write a screenplay! (I'll keep you posted.)

If you liked STOP THE WEDDING! and feel inclined to leave an Amazon review, I would appreciate it very much.

And are you signed up to receive notices of my future book releases? If not, please drop by my website, www.stephaniebond.com and join my email list. I promise not to flood you with emails and I will never share or sell your address. And you can unsubscribe at any time.

Also, although I can't count the times this book has been edited and proofed, I am human, so if you do spot a typo, please email me at stephanie@stephaniebond.com to let me know! Thanks again for your time and interest, and for telling your friends about my books. If you'd like to know more about some of my other books, please see the next section.

Happy reading!
Stephanie Bond

OTHER WORKS BY STEPHANIE BOND

Romances:

ALMOST A FAMILY—*Fate gave them a second chance at love...*
LICENSE TO THRILL—*She's between a rock and a hard body...*
THREE WISHES—*Be careful what you wish for!*
THE ARRANGEMENT—*Friends become lovers...what could possibly go wrong?*

Humorous romantic mysteries:

OUR HUSBAND—*Hell hath no fury like three women scorned!*
KILL THE COMPETITION—*There's only one sure way to the top.*
I THINK I LOVE YOU—*Sisters share everything in their closets...including the skeletons.*
GOT YOUR NUMBER—*You can run, but your past will eventually catch up with you.*
PARTY CRASHERS—*No invitation, no alibi.*
WHOLE LOTTA TROUBLE—*They didn't plan on getting caught...*
IN DEEP VOODOO—*A woman stabs a voodoo doll of her ex, and then he's found murdered!*
VOODOO OR DIE—*Another voodoo doll, another untimely demise...*
6 ½ BODY PARTS—*a BODY MOVERS series novella*
BUMP IN THE NIGHT—*a short mystery*

Nonfiction:

GET A LIFE! 8 STEPS TO CREATE YOUR OWN LIFE LIST—*a short how-to for mapping out your personal life list!*

Made in the USA
Lexington, KY
13 April 2013